Grading With A Gargoyle

Slaymore Academy

Book 2

Sedona Ashe writing as Darci R. Acula

Starling Dax

Copyright © 2024 by Sedona Ashe

Gobble Ink, LLC

www.sedonaashe.com

Cover artwork by Alex Calder

www.addictivecovers.com

Interior artwork by Cauldron Press

www.cauldronpress.ca

A huge thank you to-

Allison Woerner for Alpha Reading.

Maxine Meyer for Copy Editing.

Imogen Evans for Proofreading & Editing.

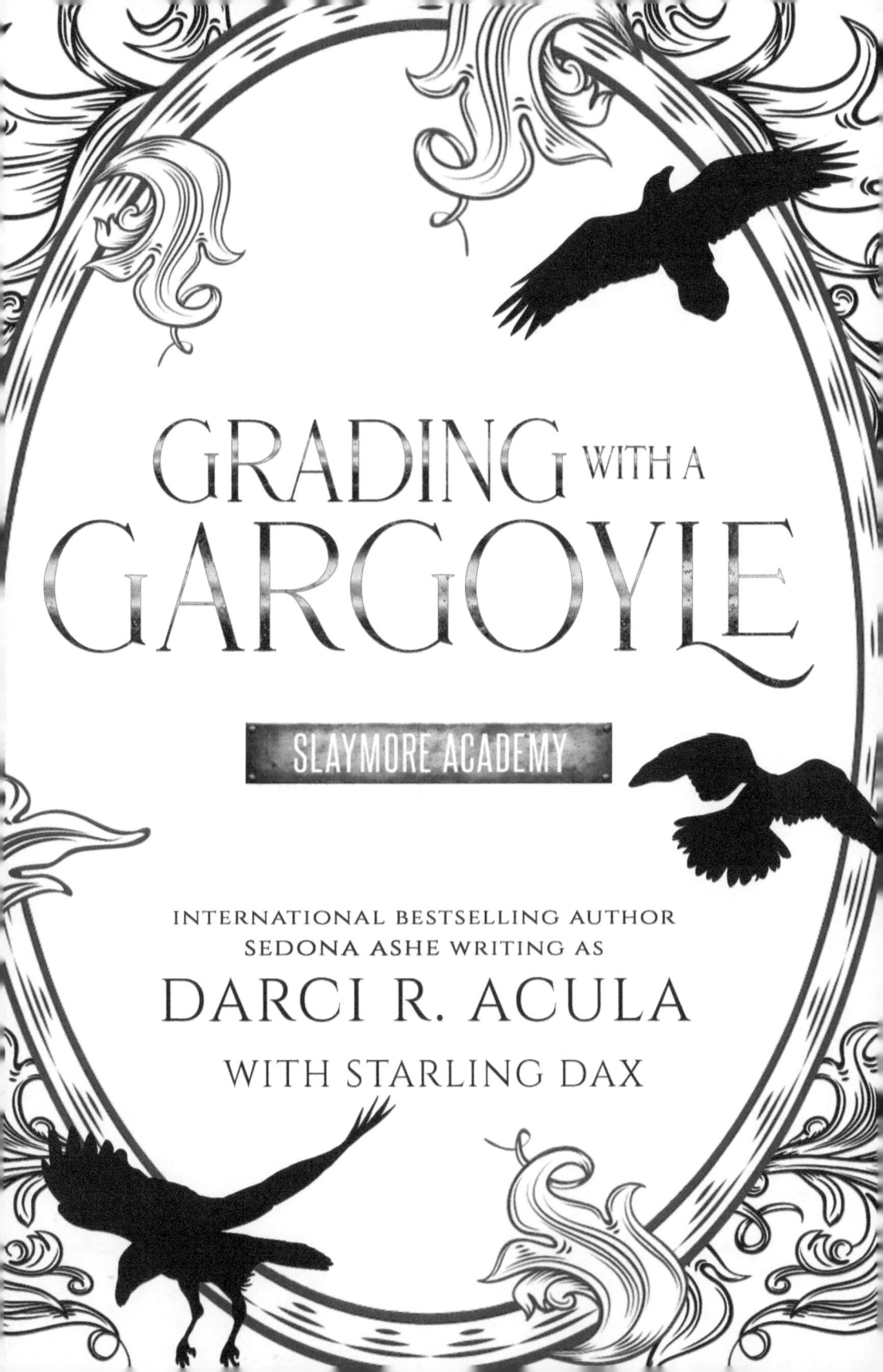

GRADING WITH A GARGOYLE

SLAYMORE ACADEMY

INTERNATIONAL BESTSELLING AUTHOR
SEDONA ASHE WRITING AS

DARCI R. ACULA

WITH STARLING DAX

CONTENTS

CHAPTER I

VELA

S laymore.

    I tried not to cry as my parents led me up to the front lawn. Crying would only show them their decision to send me here had been logically flawless. Yet the very fact that we were at Slaymore told the world loud and clear: Vela Kyanite was a failure.

Gargoyles didn't attend interspecies colleges.

But my parents had deemed me unready for a gargoyle university. According to them, Slaymore was the next best thing.

"It is the most prestigious of the interspecies schools, and there is even a gargoyle on campus," my mother had said while explaining their decision last week.

Once my parents decided Slaymore was the best choice, that was the end of the discussion.

The headmaster's house looked as though several generations of headmasters had tried to build a Victorian structure, only none of them could quite agree on the blueprints. Glancing up, I studied the imposing building.

It rose to dizzying heights, the various levels occasionally growing thinner and sometimes thicker. Balconies ran all the way around each floor, supported by carved stone pillars.

Lowering my eyes, I let my gaze travel around the students scattered around the lawn, carrying suitcases and campus maps. They hugged their parents goodbye while looking at Slaymore with shining eyes. Their mothers and fathers were tearful, probably from pride, sorrow, or some other emotion—all of which gargoyles weren't supposed to feel.

"And I'll send you minnows every week," a mermaid mother sniffled.

Her daughter rolled her eyes. "They have minnows here, Mom."

"Not like the minnows I make." The mother dissolved into tears as her daughter flung her arms around her neck.

"Vela." My father's voice caused me to jump, and my cheeks burned as I realized I'd been staring.

Staring… and maybe wishing.

"You aren't feeling maudlin, are you?" My father emphasized the word *feeling* as though it was vulgar.

"Of course not." I smoothed down the front of my skirt, a sensible gray thing that looked a lot like the uniform I'd worn in grade school.

"Don't think we haven't noticed your troubles as we arrived here," my mother's voice was crisp and steady, as though reading an academic paper.

There wasn't even a hint of an emotional wobble, but I wasn't surprised. My mother was the perfect gargoyle. She could also sniff a lie on me from a mile away.

Rather than deny it, I tried to change the subject. "Are we certain I can't go to a gargoyle institution?"

"Unacceptable emotional displays are precisely why you're enrolled here." My father had a deep voice that perfectly fit his tall figure.

On the Slaymore campus, he didn't have to bother hiding his deep gray skin. The wind toyed with his dark hair, pulling it away from his light green eyes. "By the time a gargoyle is your age, she ought to have complete control over her emotions. That you cannot reflects poorly upon you and the entire Kyanite family. If you do not correct this failing, you will be excluded from activities for which you are deemed unready, and judging by your current emotional display, you will be excluded from everything in gargoyle society."

I wiped under my eyes, trying to collect my unshed tears while making it look like I was merely wiping away makeup—which was yet another thing gargoyles saw as frivolous and illogical.

"Slaymore will give you two valuable opportunities," Mother added. "First, take this time to understand the people of the world and see how you can best protect them when you are assigned a city of your own. Second, this will be a good time to observe how their pointless emotions ruin their lives. If you can fully embrace the gargoyle way by the time you graduate, we will continue with your city assignment. Otherwise, we will have to pursue more... drastic measures."

I carefully squashed my shudder at the idea of "more drastic measures."

No one wanted to talk about it, but we all knew what it meant. The collar.

A magical binding that would be fastened around my neck and would turn me to stone for a hundred years. During that time, I'd be unable to move from the same spot, yet I'd be conscious of everything that went on around me.

My high school teachers and advisers had claimed it was an effective way to get into the gargoyle mindset when they first suggested the idea to my parents. But they'd carefully avoided mentioning it was also torture for a gargoyle.

"Professor Carnelian has agreed to meet you here, in front of the headmaster's house, at nine o'clock this evening for your first lesson. We have told him you are punctual and obedient, although prone to fits of emotion. You will not make liars of us."

"No, Father." I nodded obediently.

And I wouldn't. Professor Carnelian and his lessons were all that stood between me and the dreaded collar. He was an old gargoyle and something of an outcast in the community. But he still commanded enough respect that my parents had written to him about my problem and had accepted his offer of help.

"We expect to see progress when you return for the holiday closures." Mother stuck out her hand. "Your father has agreed to visit so that we might assess you together."

I shook her hand, hoping she didn't detect the slight tremor in mine. My parents had spent perhaps three weeks together in my entire life.

Gargoyles didn't mate for life. Instead, we mated for a purpose. They each had their own city to guard, so after they did the deed, the only thing they'd communicated about was me.

Shaking Father's hand next, I then stood quietly as Mother and Father shook hands with each other. This was as emotional as it got in gargoyle families. I hated it, but that type of mindset landed me at Slaymore instead of a gargoyle college.

Swallowing the remnants of my emotions and mustering the most expressionless voice I could manage, I murmured, "Thank you for eighteen years of parentage."

"Raising offspring has been an interesting experience," Mother replied.

"We greatly anticipate news of your success here," Father said.

And that was that.

While everyone else exchanged *I love yous* and *call every days*, my parents turned away from me, walked across the lawn, and climbed into their hired car. They didn't turn around once. That would have been sentimental, after all.

I wasn't surprised, but I still wanted to cry. However, there wasn't a chance I wanted to start my Slaymore career

with an emotional breakdown. I could do better than that…
I had to.

Because if I wasn't better in four years, I had a hundred years of prison to look forward to.

Opening my campus map, I studied the various buildings. We had an orientation in fifteen minutes, and it wouldn't do to be late.

As I decided which direction was most efficient, I heard a voice so cold and brisk I thought another gargoyle family had arrived.

"There will be no need to call."

Curious, I looked up. The family stood nearby, a father and mother with two identical young men. The parents were dressed in fine morning suits with crisp linen shirts and satin jackets the color of the late summer sky.

One twin was dressed in a black suit jacket with a red tie, while the other wore jeans and a polo shirt. A small suitcase sat on the ground next to the latter.

"I'm sure there won't," said the polo-shirt guy in an equally neutral tone.

He lacked the gray skin most gargoyles sported, though I supposed he could be one of the rare white marble families. His pale face was almost corpse-like, with a pointed chin and nose.

Wavy black hair flopped over his eyes, and he pushed it out of his face with an elegant long-fingered hand. His full lips were turned down in a frown.

Our eyes met.

And I sucked in my breath when his glinted red, like a burning fire.

I almost looked away, embarrassed to be caught staring. But that wasn't what Mother or Father would do. Instead, I lifted my chin and regarded him coolly as though he didn't impress me.

It was a lie. He was breathtakingly beautiful in a sharp, melancholic type of way.

"Mother. Father. Thaddeus." He tilted his head at them.

He hadn't offered them so much as a handshake.

I filed that away for the next time I saw my own parents. They'd be impressed at the lack of physical contact. My heart ached as I wondered for the millionth time what it would be like to get a hug. It was something I'd never know.

As his family turned away, I decided they were *not* gargoyles. Perhaps there were other species like us who preferred to put logic and reason first. Maybe there was more to learn here at Slaymore than I'd anticipated.

Hopefully, that would prove to be the case.

I was determined not to be a failure. Folding my map, I headed behind the headmaster's house. If I used my time at Slaymore wisely, I could impress even the most stoic of my kind.

CHAPTER 2

VELA

Three and a half years later.

"To Kaya!" I solemnly lifted my glass.

"To Kaya," my roommates echoed, enthusiastically clinking our glasses together and causing our bright green appletinis to slosh over the rims.

We took a sip of our drinks, and I tried not to react to the sour taste of the appletini puckering my mouth. Kaya, the petite fairy we were celebrating, turned a delicate shade of pink and tucked her white-blonde hair behind her pointed ears.

"We're so proud of you, babe." Meribeth downed her appletini in one go and refilled her glass from the pitcher on the table.

I'd never seen Meri turn down a drink, but I'd never

seen her drunk, either. It probably had something to do with her being a harpy who stood over six feet tall on her taloned feet. Heck, even with wings tucked tight against her back, her shoulders were so broad she sometimes had to enter a room sideways.

"I didn't tell you this, but when you applied to Vitaly & Sons, I did the numbers, and you only had a 4 percent chance of landing the internship," our final roommate, a nerdy witch named Meg, retorted.

Meg was curled up on her favorite dining chair, with her knees tucked under her delicately pointed chin. She toyed with a crystal pendant at her throat and slowly turned her appletini this way and that so that it caught the light and sent tiny slivers of bright green light across our table.

"Well, I'm glad you didn't tell me!" Kaya's bright blue eyes widened. "I was nervous enough during the interview rounds without knowing those odds!"

"Look at you, Meg! You're making progress!" Meri praised, lifting her glass toward the witch. "Remember, all data is equal—"

"—but some data is best kept to myself. I know." Meg stuck out her tongue at the harpy, then took another sip of her drink.

"When will you start, Kaya?" I asked.

"As soon as we graduate. I walk, I pack, then I'll go straight to the big city. My mom's going to help me find an apartment and get settled in." Kaya's lips curved into a quiet smile over the top of her glass.

Unlike Meg and Meri, Kaya was more reserved.

Though from the fidgeting and fluttering of her gossamer wings, she appeared to be on the verge of exploding from pent-up energy. And she deserved it. Vitaly & Sons was one of the most prestigious law firms in the paranormal world.

"I can't believe you know what you want to do with your life." Meri propped one enormous taloned foot up on a spare chair.

Our dining room was a mishmash of furniture we'd rescued from other students' apartments when they moved out. We had three chairs—one covered in green brocade, one ugly, brown-checked folding chair, and a luxurious leather armchair we called the throne.

Kaya got the throne tonight as she was the woman of the hour. Our table was a beat-up, wobbly, circular thing with a summoning board crudely burned into the middle. Meg had insisted we take it when some of her witchy sorority sisters graduated and moved out.

Even the glasses we were drinking from were from different sets. Instead of lamps lighting the room, we had candles set everywhere, enchanted by Meg so that nothing caught fire.

The kitchen was cluttered with plants, liquor bottles, and ceramics Meri had made for her art minor. It was the complete opposite of the way I'd grown up.

My mother's house had been bland and bare since all decor was seen as frivolous. I hadn't even been allowed to paint my room a different color.

"I've known what I wanted since I was a kid." Kaya

shrugged. "What can I say? I like to argue, and I'd like to get paid for it."

"And you're going to put in a good word for me so I can get a job in your IT department," Meg added.

Kaya lifted her hand, and the girls high-fived.

"Even the little witch knows what she'll be doing." Meri scrunched her nose and gave me a look. "I need another year at Slaymore to figure things out. Maybe I should flunk all my finals."

I knew exactly what I would be doing, but my future didn't feel nearly as bright as Meg and Kaya's. It was a solid future, and I knew that as a gargoyle, I should prefer that. We didn't have patience for flashy, passionate careers.

In fact, it was rare for a gargoyle to have any sort of career outside of guardianship. We exist to guard cities and townships from threats, both natural and unnatural. In some rare cases, gargoyles like my mentor, Professor Carnelian, guarded individual buildings and the important people inside them rather than a city.

When I graduated—provided I could show my parents and the Gargoyle Council I was a proper gargoyle who'd gotten her crap together—I would be assigned the guardianship of a city.

Most likely, I'd be assigned to a new city that didn't have a gargoyle or to a city whose previous gargoyle guardian had been promoted to a larger city. In some rare cases, a gargoyle might be deemed unworthy to continue guarding their city, and they would be replaced.

I wouldn't get to choose my city or have a say in where

I'd like to live, and I wouldn't be allowed to dislike it. Those were the facts, and I shouldn't feel either positive or negative about them.

This was the gargoyle way, and I had to accept it.

"You're not going to flunk your finals. You always threaten to, and you never do." Meg clucked her tongue at Meri. "Besides, you don't have to know exactly what you want right out of college. Heck, my mom's still experimenting."

"And you complain about her at least once a week!" Meri pointed out.

Meg laughed, nodding at the truth of the statement, and they clinked glasses again.

The clock over the mantlepiece chimed one.

Grimacing, I gulped down the rest of my appletini. "I have to go stone up."

Meri sat straight up. "Yas, girls! Let's get stoned!" Then her face fell. "Oh, you didn't mean like that. Did you?"

I nearly giggled but stifled it—barely. The only outward sign of my amusement was a brief quirk of my lips.

Honestly, my control was impressive, considering I was two appletinis in. However, to be a satisfactory gargoyle, I shouldn't have found her comment amusing at all.

Three years into Slaymore, I was still struggling with control. Maybe I was a lost cause. At this rate, my graduation gift was going to be a collar and a hundred-year time out. That thought sobered me up in a hurry.

"I am not responsible for anything you might do while I'm gone," I pointed out, voice flat.

"Spoilsport." Meri huffed, clicking her long talons on the floor.

Ignoring Meri's pouting, Kaya slid out of her chair and came around the table to give me a hug. I was short, but at five-foot-one, Kaya was the tiniest of us, and that was tall for a fairy.

"Thanks for celebrating with me, Vela." She squeezed me tight.

"Don't trash the place while I'm gone," I replied.

Among the roommates, I was definitely the tidiest. It was probably because I came from an austere living culture, which meant I hardly had any mess to make.

Plus, gargoyles took the logical route toward cleaning—when there was a mess, the mess got cleaned. It had taken the others a long time to convince me I didn't need to wash my plate and fork the minute we finished eating.

"You know Meri will. She can't help it," Meg laughed and, ignoring my stiff posture, gave me a tight hug.

Meg wasn't much taller than Kaya, but she was more solid, an oak where Kaya was a whipper-thin willow.

"I should be insulted, but you girls know me too well." Meri didn't bother to stand; she waved me over and gave me a half-hug that would've crushed any lesser paranormal.

I left the house with the tinkling sound of my friends' laughter filling my ears. Friends.

Even now, three and a half years into my Slaymore education, it was sometimes hard to think of myself as a girl who had friends. Friends were for other paranormals.

Gargoyles didn't have friends; they had partners. Partners in work, partners in parenting, and partners in achieving various work-related goals.

I'd once confided my concerns about having friends with my mentor, Professor Carnelian. He'd leaned back in his professor's chair and considered me with his orange-red eyes.

"It is only logical to assimilate, to some degree, to life at Slaymore," he'd pointed out in his gravelly voice. "You are learning the nuances of the space you live in. When you are the guardian of a city, you will need to do the same."

"But gargoyles live their lives separate and apart from the lives of their constituents," I argued, remembering one of Mother's lessons.

"Indeed. But at Slaymore, your status is not that of a guardian but of a guarded. Your time here affords you the unique opportunity to understand a city, not in terms of streets and buildings and laws, but in terms of the people who live there. They are messy and illogical, so what better way to engage with them than in something messy and illogical like friendship?"

I found Professor Carnelian's advice to be instructive, but I knew in my gut that it wasn't an argument my parents would have approved of. Friends would be seen as a waste of time and a distraction from my goal of ridding myself of emotions.

When I'd first arrived, I'd planned to avoid becoming close to anyone, but the three women had insisted on being my roommate. And while it went against everything I had been raised to believe, I secretly loved the emotions they stirred in me.

I enjoyed their laughter and jokes—even if I didn't understand much of their humor. They'd caused me to feel anger over their bad dates, and I'd experienced joy when celebrating their exam results. Emotions felt natural, so why did gargoyles have to suppress them?

It didn't matter why. My time at Slaymore was rushing by, and soon I'd have to prove to my parents my unruly emotions were no longer an issue.

As I unfurled my wings and took to the cloudless spring night sky, I cast a final look back toward our little house, a tidy four-bedroom in a row of tidy four-bedrooms meant to house the final-year students.

I'd miss that little house when I graduated. I'd miss the Slaymore lawn, the lake, and the freaky gazebo that occasionally tried to eat people. I'd even miss the headmaster's house, as ugly a building as I found it.

Gargoyles weren't supposed to feel an attachment to things, but I couldn't deny that I loved everything about Slaymore, and it was going to break my heart to leave.

CHAPTER 3

VELA

I flew past the barriers that separated Slaymore Academy from Slaymore town, the so-called "mundane" town attached to the academy. There were plenty of mundanes living there who knew nothing of paranormals or magic, but there were also a plethora of paranormals who'd settled down in the town and made a living there for themselves.

Since mundanes weren't supposed to know about the existence of paranormals, we had to disguise ourselves as humans when we visited the town. Most of the shops were like the shops you would find anywhere else in the world, but many of the shops owned by paranormals had a hidden back room with magical items available for purchase—or a space where a girl could drop her disguise and let her wings out.

I used an invisibility spell to cloak myself as I flew into town and settled on my favorite roof. Curling my wings around me, I dropped the spell and slowly breathed out.

I imagined myself exhaling everything that made me alive, like the beat of my heart and the warmth in my blood. Then I breathed in, and the change began to ripple over my body.

Stone crept over my bare feet first, turning them to talons of dark gray marbled with a pale green. It traveled up my body until it reached my head and twisted my face into the classic gargoyle grimace.

I wasn't supposed to feel hate or love, but I hated that grimace.

For as long as a gargoyle held their breath, they would remain in their stone form. Gargoyles could hold our breaths for centuries, but thankfully, I didn't need to hold mine for longer than four hours. When the warm rose-gold hues of dawn painted the sky and the people of Slaymore town began to wake up, then I could return to my living form.

As the last of my skin turned to stone, the first of the birds arrived on the roof. Crows curled their tiny talons around the edges of my wings while curious ravens settled on my knees and arms.

A bubble of happiness formed in my chest at the arrival of my feathered friends, but I quickly popped it. I was there to be a better gargoyle, not to give in to the abundant emotions I'd been cursed with.

A week after I'd arrived at Slaymore, Professor

Carnelian had assigned me these "stoning up" sessions as a way of practicing the skills I'd need when I became a guardian. He was the guardian of both Slaymore town and academy and had been assigned to them for so long that he could keep track of much of what went on just by sensing it. This meant he didn't need to physically sit on the roof every night to watch but could move around or even spend parts of his nights in his apartment with his windows open and his senses alert to changes in the wind or his magic.

But as a gargoyle in my twenties, I would need years to grow into my abilities. The professor believed these sessions would not only help me strengthen those abilities but would help me stay connected with my gargoyle roots while living among beings who thrived on emotions and chaos.

"Living among other paranormals can be challenging," he'd said. "They suffer a plethora of emotional ailments, often without even realizing it. Taking a stone watch is necessary to ground yourself and assist you in remembering your purpose. It is an important skill, and should the Gargoyle Council wish to see a demonstration of your abilities before assigning you a city, these practice sessions will improve your performance."

He had made valid points, and I'd been stoning up at least once a week since that conversation.

I wasn't sure it was working to help harden my heart. All I could think of as I crouched on the roof was how beautiful the moonlight looked as it slanted over the cobblestone street, scattering silver like coins. The play of light and shadow was something I'd never grow bored with.

The wooden sign for *Books and Brews*, a coffee shop run by a renowned witch, creaked as it wobbled in the evening breeze. I'd miss that coffee shop when I left Slaymore.

Sadness sliced through my mind. I loved guarding the city through the quiet of the night, but one of my favorite times was dawn. There was something special about watching the sky turn a golden hue as it painted the drab gray flowers in a rainbow of brilliant color as light re-entered the world.

Objectively, I knew there were other cities with cobblestone streets, beautiful sunrises, and cheerful flowers. But deep down, I knew it wouldn't be the same.

Maybe it was the happy memories I'd attached to the city. Glancing back at *Books and Brews*, I remembered the first time Meri had taken me in there. She'd bought me my first, and last, cup of coffee. There were many things I didn't understand about humans and other paranormals, but how they could drink that bitter bean water was one of the most confusing. That had been the day Meri told me straight up that I'd be moving in with her, Meg, and Kaya.

A breeze tickled my stone nose, bringing with it the smell of the sea and the memory of the time the girls had talked me into sneaking to the pier and skinny dipping.

There were thousands of cities, but I wouldn't have these memories in a new city. Sadly, I wouldn't even be able to make new experiences because my status wouldn't be that of a citizen anymore... and guardians did not go skinny dipping.

I caught movement from the corner of my eye, and I immediately turned my full attention back to my task. Watching.

Four hoodie-wearing figures came into my view. They were male adolescents, judging by their height and the confident swagger of their gait. The boys had their hoods pulled up around their faces and cinched tight so only a small portion of their pale noses and eyes could be seen.

Gargoyles weren't good with emotion, but we were skilled at picking up on body language. They were up to no good.

They came to a stop in front of *Books and Brews*, and one of them kneeled in front of the door. He pulled something long and slim from his pocket. As he held it up to the door, the moonlight glinted off the screwdriver. They were trying to break the lock.

The witch who owned *Books and Brews*, Marita, had probably warded her shop with some unpleasant spells to protect it from a break-in. Then again, she might not want to risk using magic in case it triggered suspicions about who she really was or what her powers might be.

If I were a guardian of a city, it would be my duty to prevent harm from coming to the shop in the first place. Since I was practicing being a good gargoyle, it seemed obvious what I should do.

Exhaling slowly, I let my body return to flesh, reversing

the process that had turned me to stone. Ideally, I would prevent the break-in without hurting the boys, who were also citizens of the city.

I shook my arms gently, causing the birds to take to the air, cawing in annoyance at being disturbed. The boys jumped, wide eyes searching the darkness around them.

"I told you this place is freaky!" one of them said.

His friend shoved him. "Stop being weird."

Glancing around, I noticed the tiny pebbles and leaves filling the roof's gutter in front of me. I extracted a pebble and took careful aim.

My weapon of choice in my Non-Magical Combat elective had been the bow, but I was good at hitting most targets I aimed for. Since my eyesight was best at night, I had every confidence as I lobbed the pebble.

It struck one boy just above the ear, and he released a loud curse. The other three boys stood frozen, their eyes darting around the street.

"It must've been the wind, man," his friend laughed nervously.

The boy I'd hit put a hand to his head, then looked at his fingers. "Are you crazy? I'm bleeding. Wind doesn't do that."

"Okay. Bug bite, then?" another boy suggested.

"That would have to be a huge freaking bug." His chest began heaving as he hyperventilated.

"Look, I'm almost done—" The boy holding the screwdriver dropped it as another pebble hit the door right above his hand.

I grimaced. The pebble should've hit his hand; now, Marita was going to have a scratch on her door.

The boy leaped to his feet. "Who's there?" he demanded, pitching his voice for bravado. I didn't miss the way it wavered with fear, though.

One of his friends punched him in the shoulder. "Don't ask that, you idiot! We don't want to get caught."

I hurled another pebble, this time striking one boy on the cheek. He let out a high-pitched scream that sounded more like a tween girl than a wannabe thug. He clapped his hand over his mouth.

"Dude, I told you this place was haunted. Let's just get out of here." The first boy I'd hit yanked on the arm of the guy who still held the screwdriver.

Screwdriver Boy shook him off. "Quit acting like a fool. There's no such thing as ghosts."

I had to stifle a very un-gargoyle-like chuckle at that.

With a gentle spell, I sent a burst of wind funneling down. It whipped at their hair as I tossed a shower of pebbles in their direction. A moment later, the wind swept down the street with an unsettling, mournful moan.

"Screw this! I bet the old bat doesn't have anything worth stealing anyway." The first boy shoved his hands into his hoodie pockets and started off down the road.

"Coward," Screwdriver Boy snarled as the others backed away from the shop.

"Sorry, man," one of them said, shrugging apologetically. "We're out. Stay and get haunted if you want."

"Yeah, Dave has a point," said the other as he hurried

down the street toward his friends, leaving Screwdriver Boy alone.

He looked back at the door, then looked around the empty street. Finally, his gaze drifted up to the roof, where I lingered. I stared down at him without fear. In three and a half years, I'd never been caught while guarding Slaymore town.

Calling my gargoyle magic, I pushed a sense of urgency and foreboding toward him.

You want to go home.

This isn't worth it.

This shop is guarded.

We didn't have telepathy with other species, but humans were impressionable, and it was generally easy to project feelings onto them.

With a curse, the guy shoved the screwdriver back in his pocket. Looking back at the door a final time, he kicked at the ground and cursed again before turning and running down the street.

Smart boy, I thought, swelling with pride. I might have come to Slaymore as a poor excuse for a gargoyle, but I was growing confident I would leave it with the ability to protect whatever city I was assigned. If Professor Carnelian taught classes in city protection, I'd be acing them.

A warmth started in my belly that spread all the way to my toes. I recognized the emotion. *Love.*

I loved this place.

A gargoyle was supposed to protect their city, but

feeling an emotional attachment to a place was something I'd never heard of. Probably because proper gargoyles didn't struggle with overactive emotions.

It might not be normal for me to feel something for a city, and maybe it was just my imagination, but I swear I could feel an answering swell of warmth from somewhere far below my rooftop perch. It was as though the city loved me, too.

All right, now you sound like an idiot. Get it together, Vela. I lifted my arm to run my fingers through my hair but caught myself and lowered my arm. Gargoyles weren't supposed to show outward signs of anxiety or agitation, so I couldn't afford to pick up any bad habits.

Glancing at the moon's position, I realized I should stone up again. There was plenty of time to finish this exercise.

Professor Carnelian would understand the actions I'd taken to preserve the coffee shop. But I knew if I finished my lesson too early to celebrate my small victory, he'd point out that the very act of stopping my lesson for an emotional reaction had actually caused me to fail.

I exhaled the air from my lungs, getting myself back into the proper mindset. Taking a deep breath, my body slowly turned back to stone, banishing the warmth from my belly with a whisper of regret. I wasn't alone for more than a handful of minutes before the birds flocked back to roost on my shoulders and outstretched wings.

The next hour ticked by without incident, and I was

working to ignore my growing boredom—yet another thing a gargoyle shouldn't feel—when a familiar raven appeared out of the night.

He fluttered and circled, refusing to land. His caws of panic caused the other birds to flutter their wings and watch him warily. Ignoring the others, the raven continued to circle, clearly uneasy about something and anxious to tell me.

What was I supposed to do? A gargoyle wasn't supposed to shift from their stone form at every little sound or to chat with every anxious bird.

But what if there was another problem in town? What if those boys had decided to break into some other shop?

Exhaling, I gently shook a dove off my head and held out my hand for the raven to land. He did and released three ear-piercing screeches directly in my face.

I didn't understand the nuances of bird speech, but I understood enough to take an educated guess at what he was saying. "You've... found something?"

He flapped his wings, which I took as a yes.

"Shall I follow you?"

In answer, he took to the sky and flew a quick lap around the roof, waiting for me to join him.

Pausing briefly, I cast my spell of invisibility and unfurled my wings. Leathery skin stretched over bone, allowing me to leap off the building and take to the air with ease.

My wings had more in common with a bat than a bird,

but for some reason, I'd never really gotten along with bats. Birds, on the other hand, loved me. Especially corvids.

I focused on keeping my raven friend in sight as he flew back toward Slaymore Academy. With worry growing in my stomach like a block of granite, I didn't even notice the beauty of the town as it flashed beneath us.

CHAPTER 4

VELA

I n no time, we were through the barrier, and I was winging my way over the woods on the edge of Slaymore Academy's property.

The raven headed straight to the headmaster's house. Though it was called the headmaster's house, Slaymore was currently overseen by a headmistress, and she didn't actually live there. However, the rest of the faculty lived there in small apartments divided up among the levels.

I'd been to the headmaster's house many times to have lessons with Professor Carnelian—enough times that I instantly recognized the window the raven led me to.

Landing lightly on the balcony outside, my claws gripped the ledge next to the claw marks where he often perched when he was in his stone form.

The raven tapped frantically on the glass, his feathers lit

by the soft glow emanating from within the apartment. I waited for a moment, but no one came to the window in response to the raven's knocking.

Knowing Professor Carnelian often left his window unlatched so he could climb in and out as he changed, I tugged the window and wasn't surprised when it slid upward. Tucking my wings, I poked my head into the room and glanced around.

The room was as tidy as I'd expect of any gargoyle, though it was a bit more cluttered than either of my parents' apartments. A desk sat in the corner, with a neat stack of papers in the middle of it, along with a glass of water, two pens, and a paperweight.

The room had two chairs—one for him and one for a guest—as well as a side table for drinks. The fireplace bore the marks of use, but I'd never seen him actually use it, as electric lighting was more logical, and gargoyles didn't really feel the heat or cold.

As expected, the room was empty, but a guest had clearly been there recently. A mug sat on the side table, and Professor Carnelian kept tea and coffee only for guests. The guest chair was pushed back at an angle that suggested someone had gotten up in a hurry.

Climbing through the window as quietly as I could, I tried to calm my nerves. I'd never been in the professor's living room without permission before, and it felt wrong to enter through the window like a thief.

Summoning my cold, gargoyle logic, I swallowed my swirling emotions. Gargoyles didn't have feelings, and this was the logical thing to do. I'd been notified that something was wrong, and it was my duty to investigate, especially since the problem involved another person's safety.

I padded across the wood floor. A peek into the kitchen nook told me he wasn't there. The bathroom door was open, but I found it dark and empty. That left only his bedroom.

Looking at the open door at the end of the hall, I hesitated. I'd never been in his bedroom, and it felt very wrong to approach. But did I really have a choice? What if he needed help?

Taking a deep breath, I took a daring step around the corner and gasped.

Professor Carnelian lay on the floor, unconscious and barely breathing.

The next thing I noticed was the man kneeling next to him. Before I had time to think things through, my wings were propelling me forward, and my fingers were tight around the man's throat.

He made a surprised, choked sound, but a moment later, he easily broke free from my grip and tried to push me away. It wasn't happening. The guy might be bigger than me, but I was strong. He wasn't getting away until I was ready to let him go.

I caught his arm and shoved him downward. He toppled to the floor, his head cracking hard against the wooden floorboards. Pinning his arms next to his head, I slid one thigh over his waist and straddled him.

"What did you do to him?" I snarled.

His throat bobbed, and even though his hair partially covered his face, I caught the glow as his eyes flared red. My anger and worry dissipated as though I were a balloon and someone had stuck a pin in me to release the air.

Was he using some type of magic on me?

I wasn't sure, but the joke was on him. With my emotions drained away, he'd made it easy for me to separate my emotions from pure logic.

The man beneath me twisted his body, trying to look at me. As his hair fell back from his face, I realized I recognized him.

His wavy dark hair, lean body, crooked nose, and eyes the color of fire. I'd seen him on my very first day at Slaymore Academy. Since arriving, we'd had a few classes together, but I'd never spoken to him.

"Thane?" I asked again, tightening my grip. The more uncomfortable he felt, the more likely he was to answer me. "What did you do?"

Logic dictated he was the most likely suspect, considering the little I knew so far. But some part of me didn't want to believe it.

"I did nothing. I swear it," Thane answered, his voice nearly as flat as mine. "I was visiting Professor Carnelian, and he went to his bedroom to get a book he wanted me to read. There was a thump, and when I rushed back here to check on him, I found him like this. I was trying to resuscitate him when you showed up."

"And what reason do you have for visiting Professor Carnelian at two in the morning?" I tightened my legs around his waist, wanting to make sure he knew he wasn't getting away without answering me.

"I don't see how that is your business." He arched an eyebrow. "What reason do you have for being here?"

Tilting my head to the side, I studied his expression, trying to work out what he was implying. "Are you inferring that I came here for copulation?"

Thane choked, making a wheezing sound as a pink flush traveled from his ears down his neck. I knew I would've been struggling with embarrassment as well, but whatever magic he'd worked on me had done wonders to kill my emotions.

"Gargoyles mate with the sole intention of reproduction in a Council-approved transaction. Such a transaction would never have been approved for many reasons." I continued in a dispassionate tone, "You are clearly not a gargoyle, so I will ask you again. Why are you here?"

"I'm friends with Professor Carnelian, so that's why I'm here," Thane answered through gritted teeth.

"Liar. The professor doesn't have friends." No true gargoyle had friends. The fact I had friends was yet more proof of my faults.

Thane did his best to shrug, as though he didn't care what I thought. But his eyes flared with fiery rage. "You can honestly believe what you want. I don't answer to you."

In that, his logic was impeccable. I had no power over him, but I knew someone who did.

"If you try to run, I will catch you," I hissed, then slowly moved off him.

The moment our bodies disconnected, my emotions started to come back. They were dull at first, but with every beat of my heart, they grew stronger.

I did my best to shove my feelings into a box and lock them away. This wasn't the time to deal with my panic or rage.

Moving to the professor's side, I checked his airways. He was still breathing… barely. Next, I checked for his pulse, and my worry grew when I realized how weak it was.

My stomach twisted in knots as I began searching him for signs of petrification. When a gargoyle was dying, their bodies would slowly begin to petrify. It was a natural process and not something the gargoyle could control.

If Carnelian petrified completely, there'd be no bringing him back. He would be gone forever.

Petrification usually began at the extremities, so I checked his hands and feet. I breathed a sigh of relief when I found only soft skin.

While I was hovering over Carnelian's body, Thane sat with his back against the wall, watching me.

"Seriously, what *were* you doing flying in here in the middle of the night?" He rubbed at his wrists where I'd pinned him.

"I don't answer to you." Lifting my chin, I leveled a stern look in his direction.

"Touché. Satisfied that I didn't kill him?" He laughed, and the sound caused my stomach to quiver.

What had he done to me to have my body reacting to

him like this? Was I about to vomit? I'd watched other students vomit, and it wasn't something I wanted to experience.

"No. I have no way of knowing if you are involved in this." But I knew a woman who could, and hopefully, she could set this whole mess right.

Scrambling to my feet, I reached down to grab Thane's wrist. I exhaled and concentrated. My fingers turned hard and dark as veins of green licked over my marble skin.

"Hey!" Thane said, yanking on his wrist.

It was useless. My hand was a stone cuff around him, and he wouldn't be able to free himself.

I moved toward the window, pulling him along after me. "We're going to the headmistress."

"Now?" Thane had stopped struggling and walked by my side.

"Yes. The faster we see her, the better the chance we have of saving Professor Carnelian from whatever happened. You don't have to tell me your secrets, but if you are lying, I guarantee she will have a way to get the truth from you."

HEADMISTRESS LOSIA'S small private cottage was on the other side of the Slaymore wood. Releasing my hold on his wrist and without giving him time to run, I jumped onto his back and wrapped my arms under his and tight around his chest.

"What the—" he began to protest, but I ignored him and launched myself from the edge of Professor Carnelian's balcony.

It took several hard flaps of my wings to gain altitude.

When we were safely above the treetops, I looked down at him and grumbled, "You're a lot heavier than you look."

"That's shifters for you." Thane smirked and, to my utter shock, fluttered his eyelashes at me. "I will say I enjoy being a passenger princess."

Unsure how to respond, I remained quiet until we reached the little clearing that surrounded the head-mistress's cottage. We landed next to a glassy black pond, and I set Thane on his feet with a grunt. Not giving him time to bolt, I once again wrapped my fingers around his wrist, locking him in my stone grip.

Using his free hand, he adjusted his shirt. "I wouldn't mind doing that again, but I feel you should know that the service during the flight was abysmal."

I snorted. "File a complaint."

"Could I at least have my arm back?" he asked as I dragged him toward the cottage.

"No." A light inside the cottage flickered on. Good. She was awake.

"Where am I even going to run to?" Thane pressed but kept pace beside me.

The outside porch light clicked on, and I caught the rustle of movement from inside. A moment later, the door opened, and Headmistress Losia peered out. Her hair was in a loose bun, as though she'd hurriedly tied it up, and she wore a royal blue silk robe over her pajamas.

"Trespassing without good reason is grounds for expulsion, my young friends." Her voice was as sharp and cold as a blizzard wind.

I shivered. Losia was imposing, and I bet even my mother would have been moved by her tone.

Secretly, I'd hoped that by continuing to touch Thane, my emotions would be kept to a minimum, but that apparently only worked when he wanted it to.

Ignoring my rising panic and fear, I cleared my throat. "It's Professor Carnelian." I was proud my voice only wobbled a little. "He needs help right away."

Losia didn't hesitate. Stepping aside, she waved us into the house. "Come in."

At the door, I paused to wipe my bare feet on the mat while Thane kicked his shoes off.

"You can let go of me now," he mumbled under his breath.

"Not a chance," I hissed.

"Vela, please release him," Losia ordered. "Mr. Canus won't run. And even if he wanted to, the house would never allow it. You might as well come in and have some tea while I sort out what mess you two have stumbled into."

I bit back an irritated huff and allowed my hand to turn back to flesh and blood. When Thane ripped his wrist away, as though touching me completely disgusted him, my heart twinged with hurt.

"Headmistress, I don't think you understand! Professor Carnelian needs help now. I think he might be dying." My eyes burned, but I refused to cry. "We need to get back to him."

"And I will get him help, but I must also ensure you are safe, as the students of Slaymore Academy are always my priority. Come with me."

Deciding it would only delay things if I continued arguing, I remained silent as we followed her through another door and found ourselves in a spacious, well-lit kitchen.

A circular dining table held four chairs, though the stacks of paper covering almost the entire surface suggested Headmistress Losia hadn't hosted guests for some time.

The kitchen had smooth wooden cupboards and a white marble countertop. A small oven sat in the room's corner, and a bright yellow teakettle sat on the stovetop.

Losia looked us over and nodded. "I'm going to go call the nightmaster. Meanwhile, you two can fetch your own cups while I'm gone."

She motioned to the cabinet where I guess she stored her mugs. "Apple cinnamon tea should warm you up." She clapped her hands, and the teakettle began to whistle.

With a brisk nod, she disappeared.

Leaving us alone.

My emotions were coming back to me with a vengeance, and they were... more confusing than ever.

I was angry and scared. What could have happened to

make the professor collapse? Gargoyles were robust creatures, immune to most illnesses. We could be poisoned, or
cursed, but who would want to curse Professor Carnelian?

That wasn't all I was feeling, though. My stomach was
heavy with regret, as though I'd swallowed lead. I wanted
to apologize to Thane for how harsh I'd been.

His profile was stark and rather beautiful as he opened a
cupboard, searching for mugs. Thane's eyes were hard, and
the more I studied him, the more convinced I became that
he was purposely avoiding looking at me.

He was still the closest thing I had to a suspect, I
reminded myself. There was no need to apologize until I
knew an apology was warranted.

Grabbing the handle of another cupboard door, Thane
pulled out a bright green mug with a dragon for a handle.
He frowned as he turned it, and I read *I HEART
GRANDMA* written in a childish font on the side of
the mug.

Headmistress Losia was one of the earth's most famous
dragons and one of the first of her species to attend Slaymore Academy long ago. It was odd to think of the often-
stern headmistress as having grandchildren, but I liked
knowing she wasn't alone.

Suppressing a smile, I stepped forward and picked a
mug of my own from the cabinet. It read, *MONDAYS, AM I
RIGHT?*

"Well, it isn't wrong. I hate Mondays." Thane didn't
wait for my response. Instead, he motioned for me to get
the teakettle.

I hesitated, looking at the teakettle. "What about the tea bags or steeping the tea leaves?"

"I'm pretty sure it's enchanted to pour whatever tea she told it to," Thane explained. "Shall we try it?"

I nodded. Why was he being nice to me? Less than five minutes before, he'd acted as though touching my skin burned him.

Thane tilted the kettle, and a thin, amber-colored liquid poured out. The spicy, bright scent of apples and cinnamon filled the kitchen.

"Seems you were right." Taking the kettle from him, I poured a cup of my own and brought it to my nose so I could breathe in the delicious fragrance.

Thane was watching me carefully. "I thought gargoyles didn't drink tea," he said.

He was right.

Guilt washed away any fleeting happiness the tea had given me. I wasn't supposed to be drinking tea, and the fact that he was right annoyed me.

"Well, this one does," I answered tartly, taking a long sip of my tea and letting it heat the empty depths inside me.

If he didn't owe me explanations, I didn't owe him squat.

CHAPTER 5

VELA

Losia returned from the other room. "The nightmaster is investigating the matter. Thank you for bringing it to my attention."

Now that she wasn't scowling, she seemed almost friendly and much more like the kind of woman who'd be gifted an *I HEART GRANDMA* mug. Her face was slightly too thin, but the corners of her mouth turned up with the beginnings of a kind smile. And the tiny laugh lines around her eyes seemed to indicate she smiled often.

"Please have a seat."

We sat, and at her request, I poured out the events of the evening and what I'd found when I'd entered the professor's apartment.

When I finished, Thane told his side of the story. I didn't miss the way he avoided mentioning the reason he'd been in the professor's apartment. Instead, he made it sound as though he'd just popped in.

"With all due respect, his story is suspicious," I stated bluntly. "Gargoyles don't engage in 'tea and a chat.' Professor Carnelian would never have fostered a friendship like that, as it would be a waste of time."

Losia's sharp eyes studied me as though trying to decide whether I was right about Professor Carnelian. Finally, she asked Thane, "Did you visit the professor for a specific reason?"

Something in her eyes and tone made me think she already knew the answer but just wanted to see how he would respond.

Thane ran a pale finger around the edge of his teacup. "I was taking lessons from him. Extracurricular. Since we're both nocturnal paranormals, we decided early morning was the best time to meet."

Narrowing my eyes and crossing my arms over my chest, I asked, "What type of lessons?"

I hated to admit it, but his confession stung. Professor Carnelian had been *my* mentor.

"Hellhound lessons." He looked at Losia, and a sad ghost of a smile flickered on his face. "My parents would probably rather eviscerate themselves than admit it, but I'm a defective hellhound. The Canus line doesn't tolerate defects in their offspring. I was visiting him to learn how to control my powers so I could try to fix myself."

"Hellhounds... inspire terror in others," Losia said

slowly, as though trying to remember the specifics of his species. "Sometimes loyalty, or love."

"Not me. I can't make others feel anything."

"That can't be entirely true. If I recall correctly, you need to feed off the emotions of others in order to be in balance and to survive." Losia gave him a gentle smile. "You seem to be alive and quite a balanced young man to me."

"Well, I can feed just fine. I fed off *her* just a minute ago. But if I lose control, I will burn through those emotions far faster than I should, and I'll need to feed again."

I gripped the table so hard my fingers left gouge marks along the edge. "You did what?!"

"Hey, you touched me! I didn't ask for that. You didn't even consider I might have a legit reason to see him. Hades! You're the one who flapped through the window without an appointment like some monster on a mission—"

"That's enough," Losia cut into our conversation. "We don't use the m-word here, you know that. You're both adults. Act like it."

She tapped her fingers on the table, pursing her lips. "Vela has been visiting Professor Carnelian since she arrived at Slaymore. Whether she wishes to discuss the contents of her lessons with you is her business, but it was all arranged and approved, whereas Carnelian never spoke to me about mentoring a hellhound. What exactly does he provide to you as a mentor?"

Thane threw me a dirty look, and I fought the ridiculous urge to stick out my tongue at him. I couldn't deny it was unfair that he had to explain himself when I did not. But I was still annoyed at the conflicting emotions being around him stirred in me, so I didn't feel too bad about it.

"I need to learn how to enhance emotion and practice draining the emotions from others. Then, I can work on controlling the emotions so I don't burn out and need to feed again. We both agreed that it was wrong to practice on other Slaymore students."

Thane took a long drink of his tea before continuing. "Professor Carnelian suggested that the most logical solution was to practice on him since gargoyles don't have the same problem with emotions as the rest of us. Trying to get him to experience emotions was a challenge and a true test of my abilities."

I glared into my tea, hating that he was making sense. It seemed like I'd have to apologize for jumping to conclusions after all.

Losia seemed to be thinking along the same lines. "Did you practice any magic with him tonight?"

"No. I'd just gotten there. We were discussing my progress... well, more like my lack of it. The professor recommended a book on emotion and psychology, and he went into his bedroom to get it. That's when it happened."

"Hm." Losia frowned, but before she could say more, a knock came at the door.

She stood, and I did as well, but she waved for me to sit back down. "Finish your tea, I'll take care of that." Her tone made it clear that I was not to follow.

Sitting back down, I took another sip of the soothing tea. I closed my eyes and tried to pretend I was back in my own house, the professor was fine, and I wasn't fighting the urge to admire Thane's hauntingly beautiful face.

"So, what were you studying with him?" Thane asked.

I opened my eyelids. "There is no logical need for you to have that information."

My voice was more clipped than I'd intended, thanks to the flutter in my stomach caused by his glittering ruby gaze. Why did he have to be so beautiful?

"It might make me dislike you a little less." Thane lifted a shoulder in a half-shrug.

"Whether you like me or not is irrelevant," I told him, hoping to end the conversation.

If he stopped talking to me, maybe the strange warmth in my chest would go away.

He chuckled without humor. "I suppose you have a point."

The front door closed, and Losia returned. "Thank you both for coming to me immediately. Professor Carnelian has been moved to the healing house, and your quick actions may save his life."

"Do they know what happened?" I asked, my throat tight with hope and worry.

"Both of you are absolved of any culpability in this matter," she replied. "I recommend you go home and rest."

She'd avoided my question. "Will he be all right?"

"Can we see him?" Thane asked.

Losia pushed her shoulders back and tightened the tie of her robe. For a moment, she seemed larger, her teeth sharper, her eyes keener, and I knew I was seeing the hidden form of the dragon beneath her human form.

"It's time for both of you to go home. I have another matter that requires my urgent attention, and I simply don't have the time to stand here answering questions. Your concern for Professor Carnelian's health is touching, but there's nothing you can do, and I cannot disclose the details of his recovery. Good night."

Defeated and knowing she wasn't going to share any more information, we headed to the door.

Stepping outside, I was met with the bite of the crisp morning air. Thane stopped just long enough to shove his feet back into his Converse shoes before following me outside. Needing to get away from Thane so I could clear my mind, I made my way down the little dirt path that wound through the forest.

Feet thudded on the dirt behind me. "No flying?"

"Don't feel like it." I wanted time to think.

Losia hadn't assured us that Professor Carnelian would be all right. Did that mean he was in real danger of dying? Nothing about the last few hours made any sense.

"I thought gargoyles didn't feel." Thane playfully bumped his shoulder against mine.

Stopping, I turned to face him. "I'm defective. You probably understand how that feels."

He'd been forced to reveal his secret. It was only fair that I did the same. I told myself that my willingness to share was from a sense of fairness and had nothing to do with the pull I felt toward him.

46

He merely blinked at me, his fiery eyes glittering in the dark morning light.

I sighed, knowing I owed him more. "I apologize for handling you roughly and for making assumptions. My actions were logical, considering what I knew at the time, but I understand that, as a result, your boundaries were likely overstepped."

"An unusual apology." Thane cocked his head to one side, studying me. "But at least you gave it. In your position, I probably would've come to the same conclusion. Now, what do you say we find out what really happened to Carnelian?"

I wasn't sure what he meant. "We know what happened. He collapsed."

"But we still don't know why," Thane argued.

"Losia will find out." I shifted my weight from one foot to the other.

I just wanted to go home where I could think through all this mess.

"Yeah, and she won't tell us anything."

"She has to follow the rules," I said, trying to use logic. "Rules that are in place for a reason."

Thane stared at me. The firelight glow of his eyes sent a trickle of heat through me. What was going on with me? Was I coming down with a fever? No, gargoyles didn't get human ailments like fevers... so why was I feeling so strange?

"He could have died tonight." In the moonlight, Thane's cheeks resembled finely cut stone. "What if it's some new gargoyle ailment the healers here don't know about? I mean, how many gargoyles live here at Slaymore?"

"Just the two of us," I admitted.

The idea of investigating sounded more and more appealing. It was because of Thane's logical approach to the situation, I told myself. And it had nothing to do with my curiosity or concern... both of which were very un-gargoyle-like traits.

Thane must have sensed my weakening resistance because he pushed a little more. "I mean, isn't this part of your job? To safeguard the people of your city?"

"It's not my job because I'm not the guardian of Slaymore," I replied absently, looking back at the house.

Losia had been trying to hide it while she gathered information from us, but she'd obviously been concerned. That meant whatever was going on must be serious.

She also didn't want to share details, given the way she'd herded us out. Would she call for the Gargoyle Council to send a representative to examine Carnelian? Or would she try to fix this problem herself?

"You care about him, don't you?" Thane's voice took on a note of pleading, and I didn't like the way my heart gave a hard thud in response.

"I believe we've already established that I'm defective in that regard." I looked at the ground, adding in a whisper, "You don't have to keep rubbing it in."

"Caring about other people is defective, huh?" Thane made an odd noise in the back of his throat that had me peeking at him through my thick lashes to see if he was okay.

"Maybe you gargoyles are on to something. My life would be a lot easier if emotions and feelings didn't exist." He looked up at the stars sprinkled across the indigo sky.

His lips turned down in a frown, and a muscle in his jaw flexed. He was upset, and I wanted to fix it but didn't know how.

I reached out my hand to touch him but caught myself. What was I doing? I'd never tried to comfort a male before.

Granite! I couldn't remember ever willingly initiating physical touch beyond a handshake with anyone—not even my roommates, and I considered them friends.

Realizing Thane was staring at my outstretched hand, I belatedly turned it and offered a handshake... the world's most awkward handshake. "Fine. I'm in. Let's investigate what happened."

Thane looked at the hand as though partially afraid I might turn to stone and capture him again. Finally, he clasped it. His grip was confident and strong, his hands surprisingly rough.

I wasn't sure what I'd been expecting. Perhaps something softer, like the hands of a scholar, to match his willowy build. His skin against mine sent shivers all the way up my arm.

When he released my hand, I turned it slowly, trying to understand what was wrong with the tingling limb.

"Meet me tomorrow by the lake, 7 a.m. We can make

plans." Without waiting for my response, he turned and set off into the trees.

Gargoyles should be above feeling awkward, but I wasn't. I didn't want to follow a half step behind him, through the woods, and on to wherever he called home like some sort of creepy stalker. But I needed space from him and didn't think I could manage more conversation while my mind was spinning with anxiety and confusion.

That left me with only one option. Stretching my bat-like wings, I jumped. Three powerful pumps of my wings got me above the trees and into the sky. The air up there was even sweeter than that on the ground and cold enough to sting my nose. I let my feet graze the tops of the trees as I passed over the woods that surrounded Losia's house.

Slaymore—the *feel* of it—seemed to fill me.

It made no sense, but it was as though I could sense every stone in the town and academy. I even thought I could hear the trees and plants growing.

Magic vibrated in the air all around me, lifting my wings and my spirits. My anxiety eased, and a sense of calm seeped through me. Maybe I had a purpose beyond becoming a 'real' gargoyle like my species demanded.

For the first time in my life, I knew what hope felt like.

CHAPTER
6

VELA

T he next morning, I quietly made my way outside
and soundlessly closed the door behind me so I
wouldn't wake my still-sleeping roommates. The
day was sunny and cheerful because clearly, the weather
was a jerk who didn't care that someone had almost died on
campus the night before.

Dew glinted off the long grass covering the lawn, and
the saltwater lake in the middle of the campus sparkled as
fish, mermaids, and various tiny paranormal creatures
splashed in its cool depths. Other than the mermaids, who
were notoriously early risers, Slaymore remained quiet as
her students slept off the previous night's parties, dances,
and late-night study sessions.

True to his word, Thane waited next to the lake. He

looked as though he hadn't slept and wore the same jeans and shoes he'd been wearing the last time I saw him.

There were dark smudges beneath his eyes, and his ruffled hair stuck out at the back of his head. My palm itched with the insane urge to pat it down for him. Only because gargoyles liked order... and not at all because I wondered what his hair would feel like running between my fingers.

"There you are," he said, as though it were long past seven o'clock and not three minutes to. "Ready to go?"

"No," I replied, my wings fluttering restlessly at my back. "I thought we were making a plan? Before we go anywhere, I prefer to know where we are going and why."

"I already made one." Thane rubbed his jaw.

He hadn't shaved this morning, either, as evidenced by the dark stubble that I found more than a little bit attractive.

What is wrong with you, Vela? Gargoyles don't feel attraction, and outward appearance has no bearing on who you are partnered with for reproduction.

So why had that warm glow started inside me again as soon as I'd spotted him at the lake's edge waiting for me?

"We're going to see Carnelian. If he's awake, maybe he can tell us what happened." Without waiting for any type of response, he turned and headed toward the mansion that housed the administration and healing wing.

I fell into step beside him, growing irritated that he had made himself the de facto leader of our operation. "I thought we were doing this together?"

Thane's brow creased, and he shot me a confused look. "We are."

"But you didn't consult me on any of this," I pointed out. I liked his plan, but that didn't mean I liked being left out of the decision-making process. "Working together means we have to talk."

"Look, it may not be the most fun plan, but it is the most logical. Do you disagree?" Thane shoved his hands into his coat pockets and stared straight ahead as we walked.

For the millionth time, I wished I could abandon people altogether and find a nice spire to lurk on for the next decade or two. Gargoyles struggled with interpersonal communication thanks to our preference for brevity and efficiency. In stark contrast, most other species talked far too much. Yet when communication was most important, they failed to use it.

The earth under my feet provided a comforting presence that calmed me. That, together with the knowledge that while Thane was larger than me, I was stronger, eased my frustration. If he caused me too much trouble, I could pick him up and deposit him on a roof somewhere until he agreed to my terms.

Sighing, I nodded, even though he couldn't see me. "Just talk to me next time you're making plans. We should come to an agreement before things are already in motion."

Thane didn't reply, but I didn't mind the silence as we continued to walk toward the healing wing. It was in the only orderly part of the headmaster's house and was divided into small but serviceable rooms, each with a hospital bed, a side table, and two chairs.

With no one at the front desk of the wing, Thane and I easily slipped down the hall, checking the names on the doors until we spotted Carnelian's name. Slipping into his room, we caught sight of his grayish skin.

He didn't look good, even for a gargoyle. The skin around his nose and mouth was white, which I'd been told in my elementary gargoyle studies was an indication of illness in my species.

Carnelian's claws were visible and appeared brittle, with cracks at the tips. I wiggled my own fingertips, thinking of the claws of my gargoyle form that were sheathed beneath my skin.

He was sleeping, but it was the fitful sleep of the ill. Each shallow breath he took was labored and caused an unsettling rattle in his chest.

Thane gently touched his shoulder. "Professor?"

"Professor Carnelian?" I echoed, touching his cool hand.

Carnelian didn't respond. There wasn't even the slightest flutter of an eyelash from him.

"I think phase one of the plan is done," I muttered when it was clear the professor wasn't going to be roused from sleep.

But Thane wasn't paying any attention to me. His eyes had gone from the bright spark of fire to almost completely black, other than thin lines of glowing red that ran through them. It reminded me of cooling black lava with the cracks showing the molten red-orange lava beneath.

I wasn't great with reading emotions in others, but I recognized the sorrow in his expression, and it sent a spasm of pain lancing right through my chest. My eyes suddenly brimmed with tears, forcing me to blink hard to keep them from spilling over.

"Hold on for us," Thane bent to whisper near the professor's head. "We're going to help you. You can't leave me this way."

What did he mean by that? And why was Thane being so possessive over the professor? Carnelian was *my* mentor, and I wasn't sure how I felt about another student acting as though he meant so much.

Control your feelings, Carnelian's voice echoed in my mind. I took a deep breath. Jealousy was one of the most useless of feelings, one of the most destructive. What did it matter that my mentor was helping someone else as well? Even if that someone wasn't even a gargoyle.

Carnelian's chart lay on the table next to his bed. I picked it up and flicked through it. I hadn't attended any classes in healing, so a lot of it appeared like gibberish to me, but some words stood out to me in the notes.

Tested for traces of mercury and thallium.

No signs of scleroderma.

They were testing to see if he'd been poisoned.

"Look at this," I said, turning the chart toward Thane.

He moved to stand beside me, but before he could read the notes, a noise came from the hall. A moment later, the door to Carnelian's room opened, and a fairy nurse came in.

She stopped at the sight of us, mouth parting in

surprise. I stiffened and dropped the chart on the table with a clatter. Next to me, Thane withdrew his hand from Carnelian's shoulder.

"What are you doing here?" she snapped, her eyes moving to the chart. "That's confidential."

"We just, um..." Thane's cool demeanor had deserted him.

Perhaps he was still affected by Professor Carnelian's current state.

"We wished to pay our respects," I said smoothly, making my voice as flat and gargoyle-ish as possible. "Professor Carnelian was our mentor, and we wanted to see if he felt better this morning."

"Well, he doesn't. And the last thing he needs right now is people coming in and out and interrupting his healing process. Out with you." The fairy nurse's nostrils flared, and she flapped her hands at us. If she could have breathed fire, she probably would have.

Clinging to my gargoyle cool, I exited the room with Thane at my side. The fairy nurse must not have trusted us to actually leave because she followed us all the way down the hall and watched until we exited out a side door that led to the lawn.

I made a show of heading away from the headmaster's house, just in case she decided to glare at us from one of the hospital room windows. "Well, that didn't work."

Thane growled and kicked a rock. "Tell me about it." His voice was bitter and ragged.

I arched an eyebrow at the display. "You seemed affected back there."

An angry fire lit behind his captivating orange-red eyes, and then, just as quickly, it faded. Thane ran a hand through his hair.

"Yeah," he said quietly. "I was. Professor Carnelian—well, let's just say he has been more of a father to me than my own father. I know everyone gets sick and everyone dies, but... that doesn't mean I want it to happen now. When I thought of graduating, I never really imagined my family in the crowd clapping for me. I always thought of him being there to watch."

A kinship of sorts stirred inside me at his words. Sure, I knew my family would come to my graduation. They'd said as much when they'd dropped me off at Slaymore three and a half years ago. But they weren't any more supportive than Thane's parents sounded.

My parents wouldn't look at me with pride. They'd be waiting for the ceremony to be done so they could confirm I'd successfully completed my Slaymore education and was ready for real gargoyle life.

Although Professor Carnelian was a gargoyle, I believed he would be proud of me. He was my gargoyle mentor and the only person who'd really known what I struggled with at Slaymore. Even my friends, wonderful as they were, didn't understand me like Professor Carnelian did.

I didn't want him to die.

"Should we check his apartment?" I asked abruptly,

swallowing the lump of unwanted emotions clogging my throat.

"That would be great." Thane's eyebrows rose. "But how are we going to get in?"

I stretched out a wing, and Thane's mouth curved into half a smile. "Better not let anyone catch us."

I started around the side of the headmaster's house. "Let's go around the side of the building. We can jump right onto his balcony. It'll be like an assisted hop."

"And if someone sees us?"

"Right now, we're just two students taking a stroll and talking. There is nothing suspicious about that. Tell me more. How did you end up even meeting Professor Carnelian?" I hoped listening to him talk would distract me from the sadness crushing my chest.

There was a long pause, long enough that I wondered if my question had been too personal. Thane sighed. "It's a long story. How much do you know about hellhounds?"

"Nothing." I'd never met one before him, and I got the feeling hellhounds and gargoyles didn't exactly mix socially.

Thane nodded. "I figured. We don't get out much. Normally, we grow up and live our whole lives in Hades, the Underworld. The royal family of Hades uses hellhounds as bodyguards, and my family's bloodline is considered the cream of the crop. We've been defending the King of Hades and his children forever. My family is an elite hellhound force, if you will." He waved a hand in front of his face.

"Well, until me. The single defective hellhound in our entire family history."

He spoke the last with such venom that I was seized with the desire to catch the hand he'd waved in front of his face and twine my fingers through his. *Defective* was an ugly word. Then again, maybe that was just my perspective as another defective paranormal.

"So I was bound to this Princess of Hades," Thane continued. "Eliana."

He was bound to another female.

My stomach pitched wildly, like a tiny ship in the middle of a stormy sea. I shouldn't have been affected by that knowledge, but I was.

Shoving the uncomfortable feelings to the back of my mind to mull over later, I asked, "Bound? Like a mate?"

Thane barked a soft laugh. "No, definitely not a mate. Hellhounds would never be accepted as a mate for a member of the royal family. It's a different bond, one of a protector, not a mate."

I found I could breathe easier at his explanation and my stomach calmed. "Oh. I see."

Thane didn't seem to notice my discomfort and continued. "I took my job seriously. The only problem is, I can't do it properly. Hellhounds have this thing with emotions— we're supposed to be able to instill fear, bring out the self-preservation instinct, and heighten certain negative emotions. Basically, intimidate the hell out of you. No pun intended."

"No pun noticed," I answered truthfully, lifting a shoulder in a shrug.

Thane snorted, his lips curving into a sexy smile for the briefest of seconds. "You're intriguing, Vela the Gargoyle."

I looked away, not wanting him to see the effect his words had on me. The man was wrecking my years of careful practice at trying to feel nothing.

"I'm not very good at heightening emotions. At all," Thane admitted.

It was my turn to snort. He was definitely messing with my emotions in ways I didn't even understand, but I wasn't going to tell him that. "And that's a problem?"

Thane nodded. "Yeah. It makes it hard to protect my charge when I can't even use a hellhound's most important weapon. And then there was this incident at the Gates of Hell, where this jerk got a little too familiar with Eliana, and she wanted him to leave her alone. I drained him."

"His... life force?" I guessed, tilting my head to look up at him and finding it hard to imagine the tragically beautiful man as a killer.

"No." Thane rolled his eyes. "Nothing so dramatic. Just his emotions. I wanted to take away his lust. I thought if I couldn't make him fear me, then I could at least curb his base desires so he could realize Eliana wasn't into him."

Thane hesitated, his eyes pleading with me not to hate him for what he was telling me. "But I went too far and drained all his emotions. Permanently. He's not happy anymore; he's not sad anymore. He has no drive to work, or talk to people, or do a job, or make art. He doesn't feel anything at all. His parents made a big stink about how I'd violated diplomatic immunity laws and ruined his life."

"But didn't you ruin his life?" I asked.

Thane winced and rubbed his jaw. "He wouldn't take no for an answer and was scaring Eliana. I still believe he sort of deserved it."

I couldn't argue with that logic. Seeing how distressed the memories were causing him to be, I shifted gears. "So, how did you meet Carnelian?"

He jumped at the chance to move away from the topic of his failure. "Carnelian owed the royal family of Hades a couple of favors. We agreed they'd be squared away if he helped me. He's been teaching me about emotional control."

Thane shook his head, laughing a little. "He thinks if I can understand and control my emotions better, I will be able to use my draining powers more responsibly. And maybe I can even unlock the other powers. Honestly, I think Carnelian felt sorry for me. I've spent all the school holidays here because I've been banished from the Underworld until I can be a proper hellhound."

I didn't know what to say to that, so reaching out, I squeezed his hand in quiet support. I knew what it was like to be considered a failure. To my surprise, Thane wrapped his fingers around my hand and held it as we walked.

His skin was hot, and warmth spread up my arm and into my body. It was... nice. A perfect gargoyle would have pulled away, but then again, a perfect gargoyle never wasted time trying to comfort another person. But at that moment, I wanted to continue feeling his skin against mine, so I didn't mind being a defective gargoyle.

As we walked, I tried to figure out how Carnelian had a whole other person who was important in his life, but he'd never said jack crap to me about Thane.

Because he was teaching you how to be a good gargoyle, my inner voice reminded me.

Right. And good gargoyles didn't share the details of their lives with each other. Even my own parents didn't know the day-to-day minutiae of each other's lives.

Carnelian had been understanding about my problems, but he'd still been strict about approaching life with logic first. I just didn't understand the logic behind why he had developed a relationship with Thane.

"We're here." I reluctantly pulled my hand away from him, ducking my head so he wouldn't see the blush spreading across my cheeks.

Professor Carnelian's flat was two stories above us. A red curtain fluttered from the window I'd opened last night. No one had been in there yet to close it. Perfect.

I glanced around but couldn't see anyone around us. This was our chance. "Ready?"

At Thane's nod of assent, I jumped, hooked my arms under his, and beat my wings to give us the lift we needed. Thane's sharp intake of breath made me smile. He had been throwing me off balance since I'd met him, so it was only fair I could do the same to him.

I unsheathed the talons on my feet to grip the railing,

my claws fitting neatly into the slashes made by Carnelian whenever he landed there in his gargoyle form.

From there, it was easy to let go of Thane. Once he stood on the balcony under his own power, he dusted himself off and slid through the open window, with me following on his heels.

The apartment looked much the same as it had last night. Even the half cup of cold tea still sat on the table.

"What are we looking for?" Thane said, picking up the cup and sniffing it.

"He was being tested for poisons," I said. "Maybe if we found something…"

Thane closed his eyes and breathed deeply. I tilted my head, not understanding the purpose of his odd behavior.

"Dog's nose," he explained, tapping his nose. "I'm not smelling anything out of the ordinary. No one but the three of us and the nightwatchman have been here for at least two days. The tea was my tea, and the water smelled fine."

He moved over to the stack of papers and ducked his head, sniffing experimentally. "Nothing on any of the papers that I can tell."

"Maybe it's an odorless poison?" I suggested.

"Thallium's rather hard to come by," Thane remarked dryly. "And if it were carbon monoxide poisoning, I'd be just as ill as the professor."

I moved to the kitchen nook, eyeing the sink, drying rack, and cupboard.

"You know a lot about poisons," I remarked as I started opening doors.

Professor Carnelian seemed to favor plain oatmeal and white bread for his human meals. Pulling open a drawer beside the cutlery, I found an assortment of rocks, but nothing that looked like thallium among them.

"Hellhound, remember? I've met a lot of poisoners on their trips through the Underworld." Thane peered into the kitchen.

I shook my head. "There isn't anything suspicious or unusual in here."

"I'll take a look at the bedroom." Thane disappeared.

I'd just finished examining the bathroom when I heard the murmur of voices in the hall. They were growing louder.

Darting into the bedroom, I hissed his name, "Thane!"

"I hear them," he murmured.

We stood quietly, hoping whoever was outside would continue down the corridor to another apartment. But our eyes widened in tandem as we heard the click of a key in the door.

Thane grabbed my arm and pulled.

"Hey—" I yelped.

"*Shh*," he whispered and opened the door to the closet.

Shoving me inside, he squeezed in after me and quickly pulled the door closed, leaving us in complete darkness just as the front door squeaked open and the voices came in.

CHAPTER 7

VELA

"Have to find someone to cover his classes."

I recognized Losia's voice immediately.

"It's early in the new semester. Couldn't we shut them down and transfer the students to other classes?" I couldn't quite place the second voice.

"That's going to open us up to a lot of questions," Losia argued.

"More than having a substitute all year?" the second speaker asked dryly.

There was a long pause, and then Losia sighed. "You might have a point."

We remained silent, listening to the muffled thuds as they took off their shoes and shut the door. The floor squeaked as the pair moved through the apartment.

Closing my eyes, I bit my lip to keep from groaning in

frustration. This was why gargoyles did everything logically. No self-respecting gargoyle would be caught dead in a mess like this.

Like an idiot, I'd followed my emotions and agreed to investigate this, and look where it had gotten me! Stuck in a closet with a hellhound, praying we weren't discovered. Thane wasn't bulky like many of the werewolf shifters, but he still took up most of the space in the tiny closet.

If we were found... what sort of trouble would we be in? Would Losia think we had something to do with Carnelian's illness after all? And how would the gargoyle council react to this latest example of my inability to correct my errant behavior if they were to find out?

My breaths grew short and ragged as panic began creeping through me.

"Easy." Thane shifted, and his fingers brushed my cheek before sliding down to rest lightly against the skin of my neck.

I raised my hand to slap him away but stopped as a cool and calming sensation spread at his touch. The tightness in my lungs eased, and the fuzziness that had begun to edge the corners of my vision vanished.

Without realizing it, I'd rested my hand against his, holding him to me. As my fear bled away, my breathing became easier, allowing me to focus on willing my heart to slow its thundering beat.

He was using his powers.

And it was... nice.

No, it was more than nice. It was *useful*.

Without fear and worry crowding my brain, I could think more clearly. Yes, Losia would be angry with us for interfering, but not mad enough to suspect us or expel us.

I also realized it was unlikely that Losia would even open the closet door. If she did, maybe I could stone up and fool her into thinking that I was a statue the professor had collected rather than one of her students.

While he had taken away my distressing emotions, his touch had done something else.

It had made me hyper-aware of his soft breath next to my ear and the way my body was pressed against him. His right hand still gripped my neck, and his thumb rubbed gentle circles on my flushed skin.

It was then that I realized his left hand had slid beneath my outer coat and was pressed against my lower back, holding me to him. His touch was dampened by my shirt, but it was still the closest another person had ever come to touching me outside of my roommates.

I should have recoiled, but I didn't. Instead, I wondered what it would feel like for his hand to slide beneath the shirt and touch my bare skin.

One of his thighs was pressed between mine, and my body instinctively leaned harder into the sexy hellhound. It went against every gargoyle teaching that had been drilled into my head, but I wanted more of his touch.

Moving my hand from where it rested on his, I slid it down his chest, enjoying the feel of his lean yet muscular frame under my palm. Thane had stilled when I'd moved my hand to his chest, as though waiting to see if I was going to push him away. At my tentative exploring, his breath caught, and his fingers trailed down my throat and over my shoulder.

I found myself thinking of his perfectly imperfect nose, of the eyes that, even now, flared like molten lava in the dark. His lips were thin yet sensuous and were the most expressive part of him.

His dark shoulder-length hair covered one side of his face as he looked down at me, and I could no longer resist the urge to feel it between my fingers. Going up on tiptoe, I brushed it away from his face. I enjoyed the silken texture, forgetting all about keeping up the pretense that I was only concerned about making it orderly.

Even with his touch and magic, my heartbeat refused to calm its pounding beat. In fact, it was speeding up with each passing second. Slowly, I pulled my hand away from his hair and lowered myself from the tips of my toes... right onto his thigh.

As my body slid down his leg, the seam of my jeans pressed hard against a part of my body I'd never given thought to. I gasped, and a rush of heat shot between my thighs.

Thane leaned down, his lips brushing my ear. "*Shh.*"

His stubbled jaw rubbed my cheek, causing my insides to twist with a need I didn't understand.

Thane drew in a deep breath, and his body stiffened. His thigh muscles pressed tight between mine, and I swallowed a whimper.

"Vela," he growled my name so low that no one but me would be able to hear.

Both his hands moved to my hips. Slowly and deliberately, he rocked me against his thigh, embers glowing and crackling in his eyes as he watched my reaction.

It was then that I realized how attracted I was to this man... and how humiliating it was to know that he could smell it.

No amount of his emotion-sapping powers could drain away my embarrassment or the fiery blush spreading across my cheeks. I tried to shift away from his body, but there was no space.

Focus, I thought, and tried to listen to what Losia was saying and ignore my body.

Thane's lips brushed my neck, causing a shiver to travel the length of my body. Still, I did my best to focus on Losia's voice.

She was clattering about in the kitchen. "Don't think it's physical foul play."

"Of course it's not foul play. Who'd want to poison *Carnelian?*" said the other voice. "Let's be honest, even the staff sometimes forget he exists."

Thane's hands continued rocking my hips, and my knees wobbled. Reaching out, I grasped Thane's belt to steady myself.

"But if it's not poison, then it's something magical. And that's worse. That means whatever happened in town last night was probably linked."

I looked at Thane. His eyes flickered. Nothing had happened in town last night.

Nothing except me chasing off a few thugs, and surely that wasn't cause for alarm. Thane's shirt had ridden up slightly, and my knuckles brushed his bare skin.

A sense of delight rushed through me when it caused him to once again catch his breath. I wasn't the only one being affected by the closeness of our bodies in the confines of the closet.

"You're jumping to conclusions," said the other voice. "Slaymore town is distinct from Slaymore Academy. Not everything that happens down there has to be magical."

"But this is. I can feel it," Losia insisted. "And if too much magic attracts the notice of mundanes in Slaymore…"

"The academy might have to be moved," the other voice finished heavily. "Should I check his room?"

The thought of them moving closer to our hiding place filled me with fresh horror. Seeking reassurance or comfort, I flattened my palm on his abs, not even sure when my hand had moved from his belt.

Thane's arms wrapped around me, pulling me into the warmth of his chest. He kept his face tucked in the crook of my neck, continuing our skin-to-skin contact as he helped me control the emotional hurricane inside me.

"It doesn't look like we're going to find the answers in here. But if he's got a notebook or something in there, grab it. If it's magical, he might have written about it somewhere."

Footsteps creaked toward us, and the bedroom light

flicked on, sending a shaft through a crack in the closet door. I trembled, and Thane's hand moved over my back again, almost like an absentminded caress. Cool emotionlessness washed over me.

How could his touch make it both easier to be a gargoyle and also far harder?

"Found it," the second voice called. The muffled sound of papers being rifled filled the room. "Sheesh. Better get someone from the paranormal languages department to see if they can decipher his scratches."

"Great. Let's get out of here. The staff meeting is going to be bad as it is, and we don't want to be late."

Neither of us breathed as their footsteps returned to the front room. The sound of shoes being donned was followed by the scrape of the door as it opened. A few seconds later, it slammed, and their voices faded down the corridor on the other side of the wall.

CHAPTER
8

VELA

Silence descended on the apartment, broken only by our harsh breathing. Neither of us moved, and I kept my ear against his chest, listening to the pounding of Thane's heart.

"We should probably go," he whispered, running his hands down my back to my waist.

Rather than pushing me away, his fingers slid just under the hem of my shirt and brushed against my bare skin.

"Thane," I whispered his name.

The logical thing was to leave before we were caught, but my body had plans of its own, arching into his. He hissed between his teeth, and it was then that I noticed a hard bulge pressing against my belly.

Surprised and momentarily distracted, I trailed my fingers along the shape. "Is that a rock in your pants or—?"

Thane gave a strangled laugh and quickly pushed open the closet door so that we all but tumbled out.

"No, I'm just happy to see you." Thane gave another laugh, and pink spread across his pale cheeks. "I didn't realize you had a sense of humor lurking beneath that perfect marble exterior."

"I wasn't being humorous." Tilting my head to the side, I wondered if he was lightheaded from the limited oxygen in the closet. "And why are you happy to see me? Is it because the closet was dark? Do hellhounds not have night vision abilities?"

Thane gaped at me, my confusion now mirrored in his face. After a long minute, he barked a laugh and pulled me back into his arms in a tight hug.

Instantly, the new emotions I'd experienced in the closet burned hotter. When he finally released me, I staggered back a couple of steps as all my emotions flared back to their full strength with a fiery vengeance.

Noticing the way his nostrils flared as he took in my scent had me wishing I could crawl under the bed and turn to stone until he graduated. That way, I wouldn't have to face him.

It was a challenge, but I summoned my best expressionless mask. "I thought you could drain all emotions and leave a person unfeeling?"

Thane's mouth quirked, and he raised an eyebrow. "Before I came to Slaymore, yes. That was sort of the point of working with Professor Carnelian—to learn to not take too much."

The flare of sparks in his eyes left no doubt in my mind he had definitely smelled my desire.

Just great.

"Let's get out of here before Losia comes back," I muttered, scrubbing at my face.

"I didn't realize gargoyles were so adorable when they're embarrassed." Thane caught my hand and placed a soft kiss in the middle of my palm. "But you don't need to be. You aren't the only one affected by what happened in there."

Unable to meet his eyes, I tugged my hand away and turned to the window. They'd closed it, so I stepped forward and slid it open.

We clambered onto the roof, and I shut the window closed behind us. I left it cracked open half an inch, just in case we needed to get back in.

Without a word, I grabbed Thane under the arms. Trying not to think about the definition of his arm muscles under his coat, I leaped off the roof.

Meri had lent me a book once with a lot of smoldering glances, and I'd found the phrase nonsensical. But Thane's eyes literally smoldered and, just like in the books, it did strange things to my insides.

"So, did we learn anything new?" Thane asked as we landed on the lawn and started toward the lake again.

I shook my head. "Not much more than when we started."

Carnelian had been tested for poison, but that had gone nowhere. Losia hadn't dropped any helpful hints.

"I suppose we should investigate whatever happened in town." It must have occurred after I left, but wasn't that *also* after Carnelian had collapsed?

Or had the raven that flew to me sensed his impending crisis?

"It'll have to be tomorrow," Thane said. "I've got five classes today and won't have any time. Tomorrow, I just have one."

The day was gearing up to be decently warm, and I shucked my coat as I walked. I wore a dark blue blouse beneath, a scoop-necked one that Kaya had insisted on buying for me. Only now did I remember her telling me I looked completely jumpable while wearing it.

I had to do an internet search to find out what jumpable meant. The memory added to my embarrassment. What if Thane got the crazy idea that I'd dressed up for him?

But you don't want him to find you ugly, either. My inner voice pointed out a truth I wasn't ready to face.

My gaze traveled around Slaymore's grounds, taking in the people who were up and about. A guy had come down to lounge at the edge of the lake, a mermaid lying on the ground beside him.

He said something that made her toss her auburn curls and laugh. Then she rolled toward him and pressed her lips to his. The guy made a noise from somewhere deep in his chest and wrapped a possessive arm around her waist.

"What are you thinking?" Thane asked me.

Jumping, I realized he'd caught me staring. I'd been told

plenty of times that it was rude, but it was a difficult gargoyle habit to break.

We were good at watching, and staring for hours on end was kind of our specialty. What we weren't good at was understanding complex emotions and interactions between other species.

"What's the point?" I asked, letting my curiosity win.

His brow wrinkled, and his mouth turned up on one side. "Of… me asking that question? Of our investigation?"

"Oh. No." I waved an arm at the couple.

They'd grown more enthusiastic. The mermaid lay flat on top of her guy, her fingers working their way up his shirt.

Thane and I had touched each other in the closet, and not all of it had been to calm my emotions. I'd been left feeling overheated, uncomfortable, and embarrassed.

"I was just wondering what the point of that is?"

"Well, when two people love each other very much…" Thane smirked, looking at me expectantly.

"What?" I asked, waiting for him to continue.

Thane scratched the back of his neck. "They have sex? You know, the primal urge of all creatures?"

"But they're not having sex." We'd passed the lake now and took the path that led toward my little house on the other side of the trees.

"Which is good. Because sex on the lawn at"—Thane checked his watch—"eight in the morning would be awkward, and not something I'm keen to see. It's a pretty obvious precursor to sex."

"But why? It has no purpose in terms of reproduction. Unless the application of mermaid saliva is some sort of virility drug?"

Thane made a strangled sound in his throat before answering me. "It seems to be getting them in the mood."

He cast one last look at the couple and shook his head, smiling ruefully. "And anyway, why does it have to be related to sex? People kiss all the time for all sorts of reasons. Because we like each other, or love each other, or just want to have a good time for a little while.

"After all..." Thane bumped his arm against mine and grinned crookedly when I glared at him. "I've learned that even the notoriously stone-hearted gargoyles have feelings. And those feelings had nothing to do with reproduction."

I wanted to turn my entire body to stone, not just my faulty heart.

My wings twitched with the desire to take to the sky and abandon him on the lawn. But if I did that, Thane would believe he'd won the argument, and I'd only be proving that I had experienced something with him in that closet.

Doing my best to quash my mortification, I lifted my chin and fell back on my flattest gargoyle tone. "You have a point. While my mind may be completely disengaged from the topic of reproduction, my body, evidently, is not."

After making the admission, I quickened my step. The sooner I got home, the sooner I could part ways with him and hide in the solitude of my room.

But Thane's long legs easily matched my pace. "Look,

Carnelian spent years teaching me how to practice emotional control. Emotions are normal, and it's not wrong to feel things or indulge in your natural impulses."

"For a gargoyle, it is," I stated firmly, in a this-conversation-is-over tone.

Thane either didn't get the message, or he'd chosen to ignore it. "So how do gargoyles, you know, get ready to…"

"Copulate?" I supplied. He coughed. "Simple. We sign a contract."

Thane's coughing fit intensified until he stopped walking and leaned over to brace his forearms on his thighs. For some reason, I stopped, too, and waited for him.

When he finally caught his breath, he wiped at his eyes and wheezed, "You sign a contract?"

"Of course. A legal agreement to engage in sexual intercourse until said intercourse results in a viable embryo," I confirmed.

"That…" Thane looked dazed. "Has to be the un-sexiest thing I've ever heard."

I snorted, amused. "Well, it's not supposed to be sexy. It's supposed to be efficient."

We started off again, making our way through the slender trunks of birch and toward the cluster of houses on the other side. The sudden shade of the trees was cold, but the green-silver of the wood created a beautiful contrast with the brightness of the sunny grass behind us.

"The exchange of weird bodily fluids is what's un-sexy to me. And pointless. If you like someone, why don't you just tell them?" I mused out loud.

"You make a good point," Thane admitted as we came out on the other side of the birches.

My house stood right in front of us, all brick and timber frame, neat and cheerful. Through the dining-room window, I could see the remains of last night's party and Meri, still sprawled over the table.

"However," he added, stopping in front of me and taking my fingers lightly in his. "Have you ever tried the weird exchange of bodily fluids?"

"Um…" I stared at where our fingers met, still confused by how simply touching him could cause my skin to tingle. "No."

"Then I think you lack the experience to draw a logical conclusion." He pulled me closer, and like a thread unraveling, I felt myself moving toward him.

"Hm. Maybe you're correct." My stupid heart was beating double-time in my chest, and the strange warmth I'd experienced in the closet spread through me once more.

His nostrils flared as he drew in my scent, and his eyes burned brighter.

"Then we should fix that." Thane dipped his head, and his soft mouth met mine.

Electricity shot through my whole body. I stiffened in shock, and my lips parted as I gasped. Thane took advantage of my surprise to tease his tongue against mine. My mouth scraped over the stubble on his chin as I pressed into him, a hungry desperation to deepen the kiss urging me on.

Everywhere our skin met felt like fire and water all at once. Thane slid his fingers into my long lilac hair, holding me close. His touch sent a cascade of sensations through every inch of my body.

I made a low, involuntary whimper in the back of my throat and curled my fingers in his shirt. It felt as though I were half of a puzzle piece, and I'd finally been fit together with my other half.

Thane broke away, and I opened my eyes. He was still an inch away from my face, eyes blazing. "You have your data. Now tell me that 'just talking' is better than that."

I drew a breath and parted my lips, but I couldn't say the words. It was illogical to lie and didn't come naturally to gargoyles, but my brain was so scrambled I couldn't think of any other response.

"I'm not even going to go into that contract nonsense." Thane stepped back, giving me space I wasn't sure I wanted. "Respect for other cultures and all that, but I want my sex to be full of feeling."

I was still speechless and could only watch him with wide eyes.

Thane reached out and brushed the pad of his thumb against my lower lip. Then he flashed a dazzling smile that almost had me gasping again.

I'd never seen him smile a real smile, and it was breathtaking. He was supposed to be a hellhound, but at that moment, I thought he looked more like an angel.

"Anyway. Meet you tomorrow in the Lycan Hall? We'll make a plan over breakfast." His lips twisted in a wry smile. "And this time, we'll make the plan together."

I still couldn't muster enough of a thought to say anything but, "Okay."

Thane winked, stuck his hands in his pockets, and headed down the path toward... well, wherever he lived. I took a deep breath to steady myself.

The worst of it was, I thought ruefully, that he might be right about kissing and reproduction, too. I lacked experience, but I suspected the ache between my thighs that his kiss had caused was proof that making out had primed my body for mating.

Clearing my throat, I straightened. *Not now*, I scolded my body mentally. *Actually, not ever.*

I'd come this far on my path to being a real gargoyle. The kiss had helped me to understand humans and paranormals better, but I couldn't afford to spend my last year at Slaymore wasting time on sex and other feelings.

Still, part of me wondered if Thane would kiss me again... and if I would like it as much the second time.

Perhaps I needed a larger data set before drawing my conclusions about weird bodily fluids.

I turned toward my house.

And groaned.

Standing in the window, their astonished faces pressed to the glass, were Meri, Meg, and Kaya.

CHAPTER 9

VELA

The moment I opened the door, my ears were assaulted by hooting and clapping. Meri barreled into me, picking me up under my arms.

She swung me around twice before setting me down with a groan. "Too hungover." She leaned against the banister, looking slightly green.

The house smelled like sour alcohol and stale food. "What're you all doing up?" I grumbled, looking at their ecstatic faces.

"Cleaning." Kaya grinned at me. "I woke up when you left this morning and figured we'd better get started on the day, so…"

"And we are so lucky she woke us up, so we didn't miss this!" Meg punched the air. "Vela! When were you going to tell us you had a boyfriend?"

No. No, no, no. They had misunderstood the situation.

I'd seen enough of their boyfriends in my time at Slaymore and wasn't thrilled at the idea of another one—even if he was mine.

Meri had a new boyfriend every month, and the men she dumped always hung around the house like a bad smell for a couple of months afterward. Last I'd heard, her exes had started a club.

Meg had just had one boyfriend while she was here. They'd arrived together, and the first two years of her Slaymore existence had revolved around what she was going to do when they got married and moved back to his hometown.

Then she'd caught him in bed with a selkie. She spent the next three months crashing on Meri's couch and crying every time she had too much to drink. When she moved in with us, she seemed to perk up again.

Kaya's relationships had never been rocky, but sometimes I saw her reading romance novels and looking wistfully out the window as though she were waiting for her hero to come in here and sweep her up.

Boyfriends were a bad idea and created unnecessary chaos. Gargoyles might have this one right. Keep sex as a simple transaction; no emotions needed to get involved.

I could only imagine how bad things could go for an overly emotional gargoyle.

On the other hand... I was going to be spending a lot of time with Thane, and what we were doing wasn't exactly sanctioned by the academy. It might be smart to have a cover story.

Making my decision, I threw up my hands. "Fine. I have a boyfriend."

I was surprised the glass didn't shatter at the pitch of Meri's scream. She crashed into me again, and this time, we both went down. Lucky for me, gargoyles aren't like pixies; otherwise, she would have crushed me.

Groaning, I shoved my six-foot harpy roommate off me. "And I need a little time alone now to... process not being single."

"No way," Meri gushed, lying next to me on the floor. She stretched her arms out, and one wing flicked up. "You need to tell us *everything*."

"Meri," Kaya said warningly. She smiled at me. "Take all the time you need, Vela." A wicked gleam appeared in her eye. "But just so you know, he's *fine*."

"Too thin for my tastes," Meri proclaimed. "I'd break him like a twig."

"Well, at least you know Meri isn't going to steal him," Meg joked.

"I take offense to that," Meri huffed. She used the banister to pull herself up, completely ignoring its ominous creaking. "When have I ever stolen one of your boyfriends?"

Squeezing between them, I made my escape. A smile tugged at my lips as I trotted up the stairs to my room. Even after I shut the door, I could hear Meri good-naturedly bickering with Meg and Kaya as they resumed cleaning downstairs.

Turning from the door, I took in my room, surprised that for the first time since I'd moved in, it seemed too small. It had a single bed, a desk, and a wardrobe.

Above the desk was the string of clip lights Kaya had insisted on hanging up when she'd seen my unadorned room. According to her, my room was "like a cell, and not in a good way."

Each clip held a photo from my time at Slaymore. From moving into the house with the girls, to going to my first dance with Meri, to trying sushi for the first time. I usually enjoyed looking at these memories, but today, they caused a weight to form in my belly and left me feeling hollow.

I couldn't ever let my parents see the photos, and they'd have to be destroyed before I left Slaymore. In truth, I never should've posed for them in the first place. They were concrete evidence of my failures as a gargoyle.

Opening the small bedroom window, I launched myself into the air. I knew I should be trying to sleep to catch up on the missed sleep from the night before, but I wanted—no, *needed*—to fly.

Thankfully, because of my night lessons, I didn't have any morning classes. Pulling an invisibility spell around me, I winged my way past the academy's wards and into town.

The transformation of your flesh to stone is the act of freezing time, Professor Carnelian had told me in an early lesson. *This is what you need to do with your emotions. Freeze them before they can creep up on you and overwhelm you. At a distance, feelings become insignificant. Life as a guardian is the act of keeping a distance from everyone so you can make swift decisions without being weighed down by complicated emotions and messy relationships.*

Landing on the roof across from *Books and Brews*, I folded my wings against my back. The shop looked good. From my perch, I could see the movement of Marita's legs as she re-shelved books.

My hair whipped around my face as the wind blew in from the sea. I breathed in deeply, enjoying the familiar smell of salt and fish the breeze brought with it.

Deep inside me, I felt a rumbling vibration. Before I could figure out what was wrong with me, the ground beneath me shook. It was like a monstrous cat was purring, and the sound was vibrating bones and causing my head to spin.

For a moment, I was one with the roof and completely united with the ground. I was unable to figure out where my body ended and the city began.

My eyes widened as the cobblestones rippled on the street below. Someone screamed, and my wings snapped open in reflex.

The ground shuddered again, as though it were a sheet rippling across a bed.

Earthquake, I thought, even though it made little sense.

I'd studied the geological features of Slaymore in my lessons with Professor Carnelian. We weren't on a fault line and had never had problems with earthquakes in the past.

A memory of what Losia had said in the apartment whispered through my mind. *Whatever happened in the town last night was probably linked.*

Had something like this happened after I'd left my watch?

Books and Brews trembled across the street, several bricks cracking and falling to the sidewalk. My ears rang as people shouted in terror, tumbling out of the shops and buildings, fearing their imminent collapse.

Their panic was so palpable in the air that I could taste it on my tongue as it threaded its way into my pounding heart.

Panicking would help no one, and it went against everything a gargoyle was supposed to do. Taking a deep breath, I cleared my mind and focused.

Let your emotions freeze, Vela.

If these strange earthquakes were connected to Professor Carnelian's illness, then gargoyle magic had probably caused whatever was happening here. And I, as Slaymore's last gargoyle standing, needed to do something about it.

After checking that my invisibility spell was still in place, I unfurled my wings and drifted to the ground. I landed in a narrow alley between two buildings. On the road ahead of me, people were running past, their faces pale with terror.

CRACK!

The foundation of a building down the street split. The terrible sound sent a swarm of shrieking birds erupting from the trees and buildings and into the sky. There were so many that their wings blotted out the sun as they flew for safety.

The quakes ebbed and flowed deep in the earth, reminding me of the tide.

Or like contractions, I thought. *Or a heartbeat...*

Closing my eyes, I concentrated on the feeling beneath my feet. I sent my gargoyle magic toward it. It made no sense, but I felt as though I could touch it.

Emotions buffeted me from every side, slamming into me with a suddenness I wasn't expecting and with a force strong enough to send me flying backward into the wall.

Love, sorrow, and heartbreak disguised as hard work or hard parties. Deaths, births, and endless nights spent looking through the window as rain sleeted against the glass. Summer days spent bobbing on boats out in the harbor. Joy and fear from the wild sea.

It was as though the very essence of Slaymore town was calling to me, twining itself with my own memories of running down these streets, half drunk on freedom and futures full of possibilities.

Memories of sitting in Marita's coffee shop with a good book and a cup of cinnamon tea. Of my time spent watching as navy-blue darkness cloaked the town and tossed glittering stars in the sky like a spell. My heart swelled at the memory of the familiar prickle and weight of my feathered friends as they settled their tiny talons on my stone skin.

This was my town, the first place I'd ever truly loved

and the only place where no one had judged me for my feelings.

Reaching down, I pressed my palms to the ground, and it was as though something else reached *up*. There was a sharp snap in my mind as a link seemed to form.

Breathing in, I gathered my thoughts. I knew what to do and allowed the shift to wash across my skin, turning me to stone.

Despite the chaos happening on the surrounding streets, I was calm, emotionless, stoic. Magic flashed through my stony claws and into the earth beneath me.

Another tremor rippled through town, but the pulse deep underground had grown weaker. I sent calming magic surging into the ground and was relieved when the next tremor was even smaller.

For the next hour, I sat in the alley, maintaining a state of stability as the tremors grew slighter and farther apart. I didn't understand how exactly it worked, but I knew I'd done well.

I'd used abilities I shouldn't have possessed for many more decades. I smiled, knowing Carnelian would have praised my skill. But when I finally released my breath and straightened into my more humanesque form, I was struggling to push down my unease.

Whatever this incident was, I believed Losia was right—it had to be related to Carnelian's illness. But had my actions treated the problem or just the symptoms?

I'd never felt anything like this connection with a place

before, nor had I heard of such a thing from my parents. Of course, Mother and Father could be miserly with their information since they thought I needed to earn the knowledge of certain gargoyle secrets.

Professor Carnelian had been more straightforward with me from the start, but he had mentioned nothing about connections at this level before, either. I wished more than ever he were there to explain things.

Tucking my wings against my back, I checked my skin for any lingering gray patches before dropping the invisibility spell. I walked from the alley, and my jaw dropped at the mess the earthquake had left in its wake.

The road lay in shambles. Its neatly set stones lay scattered about as though tossed by giants. More than one house sat crooked where just that morning they'd been straight.

Glass shards glittered along the streets where windowpanes had broken under the stress of buckling frames and splintering wood. Luckily, it didn't appear any buildings had collapsed.

The next logical step would be to tell Losia what had happened.

Still, I hesitated. I'd have to explain how I knew about Carnelian's condition and why I agreed with her that the town's upheavals were connected. How could I do that without exposing myself and Thane?

But I could tell Thane. I wasn't sure what he could do about it, but we'd agreed to investigate together. And as much as I wished I could say that was the only reason, I couldn't deny that a part of me longed to be wrapped in his reassuring embrace.

CHAPTER
10

THANE

Groaning, I leaned against the shower wall. The faucet was turned to the coldest temperature possible, but the moment the icy spray hit my burning skin, it hissed and turned to steam.

I'd been in the cold shower for ten minutes, but it had done nothing to lower my temperature or ease my raging boner. All I'd accomplished was turning the bathroom into a sauna.

Hellfire! I was far from being a virgin, yet Vela had basically turned my cock to stone with nothing more than some heavy petting and kisses.

No, that wasn't quite accurate. I'd been affected by more than just her touch.

When we'd been in that cramped closet, and I'd breathed in the intoxicating fragrance of her arousal, it had taken every ounce of self-restraint I possessed to remain still. Her body was signaling its desire, and my animalistic nature was more than happy to answer that call.

I'd wanted to pin her against the wall and take her hard and fast. But her shy kisses and the halting movements of her hands as she worked up the courage to touch my body told me this was all new to her.

Hellhounds were dogs when it came to sex and we were good at it. I knew with a perfectly placed kiss here and a teasing stroke there, I could've had her begging for sex.

Yet, despite being more aroused than I'd ever been in my life, I'd backed off.

Gripping my cock which remained hard even hours later, I slid my hand along its length. I needed release, but my skin was so incredibly sensitive that I hissed in pain with each slow stroke.

This was more than just horniness or a biological need. Over the past few years, I'd been able to find no-attachment one-night stands to deal with those issues.

There were several girls on campus who'd attempted to flirt with me and made it clear they'd be open to dating or even a one-night stand. I hadn't been interested in becoming romantically entangled while here at Slaymore, so I'd politely declined or ignored the offers.

Vela had intrigued me from the moment she'd pinned me beneath her on the professor's apartment floor. And now, just the thought of another woman's hands on my body or her scent on my sheets, caused bile to rise in my throat and stabbing pain to skewer my heart.

There was only one woman I wanted to feel wrapped around me.

There was only one body I was salivating with the longing to taste.

And I'd kissed her and walked away... even though I knew she was receptive to my touch and her body had grown wet with need from our kiss.

Growing more desperate for relief, my hand moved faster along my length.

My hellhound snarled, snapping his powerful jaws inside my mind. He should've been chained and asleep, waiting to be called forward if ordered by the Princess.

As I'd come to expect, my hellhound nature once again proved unstable. He'd been restless since she'd tackled us in Carnelian's apartment. But from the moment I'd fed from her in the closet and tasted her sweet lust, he'd grown almost feral.

The need to mount her was overwhelming, but it paled compared to the mind-shattering need to make her mine. Because that's what she was. Mine.

Mine to kiss. Mine to touch. Mine to mark. Mine to treasure. Mine to protect. Mine to love.

But I couldn't have her because life was cruel and always finding new ways to steal whatever fleeting joy I found.

I'd found a mentor, someone who, in his own way, cared enough to work with me to better myself rather than just tell me how defective I was. Now he lay in a hospital, and I didn't know when he could leave- if ever.

Now, I'd found my soulmate, a rare occurrence among hellhounds. But I'd be forced to walk away from her at the end of the year.

Lifting my head, I let the spray hit me in the face as I roared my frustration. My grip tightened, and I jerked my cock roughly. I didn't even register the pain, thanks to the gut-wrenching emotional pain that was ripping me to shreds from the inside out.

Still, I could not achieve my release. Nothing was going to satisfy my hunger except the body of the tiny gargoyle who owned my soul but just didn't know it.

I focused on the memory of her body molded against mine in the closet and tried to imagine I was there again. Her lips had been soft and eager as I'd devoured her with my mouth.

She'd wrapped me in her alluring scent as her long lilac hair tickled my skin. I'd longed to slide my hands under her shirt to cup her beautiful breasts, but I'd resisted, wanting to go slow and savor her as she reacted to the lightest of touches.

Her adorable whimpers still rang in my ears, and I couldn't wait to hear her scream my name.

My heart rate spiked, and my breathing grew rougher as I relived the memory.

Wanting to give her more, I'd gently parted her legs with my thigh so that when she moved, her clit would grind against me. I'd rather have lifted her in my arms, wrapped her legs around me, and let her grind against my hard-on.

But her beautiful face, as she shyly moved against me, discovering feelings she didn't know existed, was something that would remain burned in my memory until the day I died.

A thought hit me in the face, and without hesitation, I turned off the shower. Opening the glass door, I grabbed my pants off the floor.

I quickly turned them until I found the section that had been pressed against her. Her scent had told me she was incredibly aroused, which meant she would also have been wet...

Shoving the fabric against my nose, I inhaled harshly, searching for my mate's sweetest scent.

When it filled my nose and mouth, I released a whimpering growl. If I'd been in my hellhound form, my tail would have been wagging. Closing my eyes, I kept the fabric pressed to my face as I thrust my engorged cock into my hand.

With her lust still stirring in my belly and her scent coating my senses, I came. Hard.

My body jerked, and I sank to my knees. I stared unseeing at the shower floor, unable to process that I'd had the orgasm of a lifetime from nothing more than her scent on a piece of fabric.

I might as well hand her my leash because she owned me body, soul, and mind. All I needed to do was convince her to give me a shot.

CHAPTER
II

VELA

Despite wishing I could fly straight to Thane, I had to clean myself up and head to my afternoon classes.

My evening was busy with studying and eating dinner with my roommates. They spent the entire meal trying to pry more information out of me about Thane, but I kept my answers short and went to bed early.

On a normal night, I'd be stoning up on a rooftop in town, but I was exhausted from a night of next to no sleep and the general chaos of the day. I collapsed in my bed and was asleep as soon as my head touched the pillow. My dreams were filled with buildings toppling like a child's building blocks.

The next morning, I woke up to the shrill blare of my alarm. Gargoyles are generally nocturnal and despise waking early… and I was no exception. Grabbing at the demanding machine, I smacked around for the snooze button. When I couldn't find it, I cursed and yanked the cord from the wall.

It took some effort, but I eventually summoned the willpower to roll my bleary-eyed self from the bed. I ran a brush through my tangled hair, pulled on a pair of jeans and a loose T-shirt, and stumbled down the stairs.

As I slid on my sneakers, Meg peered around the dining room door. Her eyebrows nearly touched her hairline when she caught sight of me. "What drags you out of bed before ten?" She smirked. "Or should I say, *who?*"

"Whatever," I muttered. "I'm going out to breakfast."

"Breakfast?" Meg's eyes twinkled. "If he can make you wake early and actually take time to eat breakfast, he must be special. Invite him round for dinner, okay? Before Meri corners him and drags him to dinner herself. That will be awkward for all of us."

Meg laughed at my horrified look.

"Yeah, okay. I'll ask him." Slipping on my coat, I hurried out the door before I could get cornered by my other roommates.

The cold morning air did wonders to wake me up, and the fuzz of sleepiness had almost retreated by the time I got to Lycan Hall. I even took the time to pluck a few wildflowers as I walked. Gargoyles rarely gave gifts and never anything so frivolous or useless as flowers, but I'd observed students and mundanes gifting such things as a sign of affection or devotion. I hoped it might help convince Thane of my dedication as a fake girlfriend.

Lycan Hall was a rustic place built from rough timber and full of animal-skin rugs and leather furniture. Long benches ran the length of the dining hall, and when I arrived, the room was already packed with students who all seemed to be trying to outdo each other in terms of volume.

I spotted Thane sitting at the end of one table in the corner, leaning his back against the wall and watching everyone. Someone leaped up onto one of the tables and howled. A dozen or so more werewolves joined in. The primal sound sent a shiver down my spine.

"And they call me a dog," Thane scoffed as I dropped into the empty seat across from him.

"Aren't you?" I asked, confused. "Isn't a hellhound classified as part of the Canidae family?"

Thane didn't answer. His attention had shifted to the flowers in my hand.

Feeling suddenly self-conscious, I thrust them forward. "Here. Um, we're dating now."

His eyebrows drew together, but his red-orange eyes sparked with amusement. "Is that a fact or a request?"

Nervousness was causing me to make a mess of this. I needed to fall back on logic and try to freeze my emotions. It was time to *gargoyle up.*

"My roommates saw us kissing yesterday. They assumed the—" I narrowly avoided saying *the worst.* "They assumed the obvious. Logically, the ruse is a good idea. No one will wonder why we're spending time together if we're a couple. We can investigate under the guise of... doing coupley things." I kept my voice flat and my face placid as though I were talking about a mundane topic.

Thane seemed to be trying not to laugh. "Do you mean things like making out in Carnelian's closet?"

My gaze was drawn to his lips, and I shook myself mentally. "Or taking a walk downtown to study the damage caused by the incident yesterday."

"Were you there last night?" Thane's face lost all signs of amusement, and he leaned toward me. "Were you hurt?"

It was my turn to frown. "I wasn't there last night. I was there yesterday morning—after you left for class."

My stomach jolted as I remembered my dream. "Was there another incident in the night?"

Thane nodded. "More tremors. Some of the unstable houses collapsed."

"Was anyone hurt?" I looked out the windows near the door, worried about the town twisting my insides into knots.

Turning back toward Thane, I tried to school my expression and hide the cold dread seeping through me. Without Carnelian to keep me accountable and on track, I felt more emotional than ever.

"No one was hurt." Thane's eyes studied me far closer than I was comfortable with.

"That's fortunate. I suggest we investigate the matter after class today. As a couple." I looked down at the wildflowers.

There were a few small poppies, some cornflowers, and

a purple bloom that I didn't recognize. I held them out again, more as an offering this time.

"If you accept," I amended.

Thane took the flowers from my hand, long fingers brushing up against mine and sending a tingle all the way up my arm. I bit my lip.

What if he refused me? It was his right, and there would be no reason for me to feel disappointed by it. Yet I was fairly certain I *would* feel disappointed.

"No one's ever gotten me flowers before." Thane brought them to his nose.

He looked happy, completely devoid of the sarcasm and hardness he wore like a shield. The edges of his mouth turned up, and his soft lips split to reveal the gorgeous smile that had stolen my breath the day before.

My insides turned to jelly.

Thane set the flowers down. "Well, my beautiful girl-friend. Why don't I buy you breakfast, and we can plan our next move?"

He'd called me beautiful. It was the first time a member of the opposite sex had commented on my looks. I had to admit I liked it, even though I shouldn't.

Over a breakfast of steak and eggs, we debated what to do. In the end, I convinced Thane not to go see Carnelian again. Instead, we'd head directly into town as though we were on a regular date.

"I can inquire as to the professor's health after class this afternoon," I assured him.

"Fine. But if we're fake dating, we're fake dating all the

way. I don't want just half of the experience. I'm talking dates on the beach, to the bookstore, and everything else. Wear something nice."

"I always wear something nice," I objected, then ruined it by dripping egg yolk on my jeans.

As LOATH as I was to admit it, the thought of going to Slaymore town with Thane kept me distracted throughout my entire Medieval Magic elective.

Although I wasn't the smartest student in the class, I did my best to be a model student by sitting quietly, taking notes, and answering when Professor Ash called on me. But today, my gaze kept straying to the window and the verdant grass of the lawn like a lovesick human.

I'd expected dog shifters to have hands like, well, paws. Clumsy and meaty. But his hands had been surprisingly gentle as they caressed my skin. Everything about Thane was carefully thought out and deliberate. His walk, his smile, the way he pushed his hair out of his face.

"Any ideas? Vela?"

Startled, I whipped my head to the front of the room to find Professor Ash was looking at me, one eyebrow raised. The whole class was staring at me, waiting for an answer. And I had no idea what she'd been talking about.

"Um." What had we been studying?

I flushed, my palms growing hot and sticky thanks to more unwanted emotions. A few people tittered.

Professor Ash laughed. "You know the day is too fine to be stuck inside studying when even the gargoyle's struggling to pay attention."

My cheeks grew even hotter.

"You can all go early. Stroll on the lawn and think about what you want to write about for your final paper." With a wave of her hand, she dismissed us.

Shoving my notebook into my bag, I hurried out, not looking anyone in the eye. This was *exactly* why gargoyles despised emotions.

Daydreaming about Thane's fingers when I was supposed to be focusing? What if I failed a test?

Flunking was what other paranormals did after they partied too hard. Or because they didn't know how to control themselves, or after they spent too much time mooning over and then breaking up with someone, or fighting over stupid things that ended friendships and relationships.

Time and time again at Slaymore, I'd seen people make bad decisions because of being in an emotional state. Living here had proven to me how delicate emotions made us and how strong we could be without them.

Maybe my mother was right. Emotions were useless and prevented a gargoyle from being at their best.

The sun hit my face the moment I stepped outside, and I closed my eyes, letting its warmth wash over me. And despite my misgivings about emotions only a few seconds before, I couldn't help but think about how much I loved Slaymore.

And you don't love it because it made you emotionless, a part of my brain pointed out.

No, I loved it because it was beautiful and because I'd made friends here for the first time in my life—friendships that had been forged through emotional connections.

Where would I be, and what would my life be like if I'd only ever been the prim, proper gargoyle I'd spent my whole life thinking I must become?

You'd never have been at Slaymore to begin with, I thought to myself. And right now, that seemed like a terrible fate.

I had two more classes that day, and I struggled to concentrate during both of them. At last, I was free around three, and I met Thane at the front of the headmaster's house.

"Do gargoyles eat ice cream?" he asked by way of greeting, a teasing glint in his glowing ember eyes. "Or is that too cheerful and emotional for you?"

"Plain vanilla only," I deadpanned. "Chocolate's too tasty. It makes us explode."

Thane looked away before I could catch the full extent of his smile. "Probably for the best. Chocolate is bad for dogs, anyway."

It turned out he'd asked about the ice cream because it was the first stop he'd planned on our pretend date. At the edge of town, a boardwalk ran along the beach, and over a dozen ice cream shops competed for customers despite the presence of a stiff and chilly spring wind.

Thane narrowed his eyes at each one before nodding decisively and setting off toward *Moe's*.

"Why this one?" I asked, looking at the shop that was little more than a built-up alley with a counter.

"I learned long ago to follow my nose. Now, what flavor do you want?"

He ordered himself a pecan praline, and I ordered a Rocky Road, ignoring his laughter. The cold went straight to my brain, turning it to stone as we left the shop and set off across the sand. I had to stop for a moment before my feet remembered how to walk, and Thane strode far ahead of me before he realized I'd fallen behind.

"It doesn't look too bad down here." He stopped, surveying the boardwalk as he waited for me to catch up.

Indeed, the buildings here were all still standing, though—

"Is that one supposed to lean like that?" I pointed to the *Crab Bucket*.

"Probably not. I'm guessing most of the damage must have happened closer to the center of the town. Shall we?" He offered his arm, and I took it, feeling foolish at the thrill that shot through me just from touching him through his coat.

"So something weird happened to me," I confessed as we walked. "I thought I could... feel the town."

"And that's not a normal gargoyle thing?" Thane made a complicated twist of his fingers in front of us, and the air around us rippled.

He was using a muffling spell so we'd be able to

converse without the people around us hearing the true nature of our conversation. To them, our topics would sound boring, like talk of the weather, exams, and family vacations. Only the people we spoke to directly would know exactly what we were saying.

"I'm not sure. But I've never felt it before," I admitted. "When a gargoyle becomes the guardian of a city, they bond with it on a deeper level. But this didn't feel like that—at least, not the way it's always been described to me."

"How so?" The boardwalk dwindled to a little sandy path between tufts of grass and started toward the houses on the edge of Slaymore town. Thane motioned for me to go first.

"Well, when a gargoyle becomes a guardian, we can find *anything* and *anyone*. We know where our inhabitants are at any hour of the day. We can find any building as though we were the one who'd built it. But feeling, or sensing, what's happening beneath the ground is... strange." It was more than that. It was weird, unheard of, and yet one more thing that probably made me a freak compared to other gargoyles.

"Do you think you were detecting seismic activity?" Thane asked, his expression open, with no signs of judgment.

I took a bite of my cone. "I've never been able to do that before. And I'm a pure gargoyle, through and through. It's not part of our magic."

"You're an interesting enigma, Vela." Thane stopped me as we came to a path between two houses. The main street of Slaymore glinted beyond, a jumble of cobblestone. "And you've got ice cream on your cheek."

I lifted my fingers to wipe it off, but he caught my hand with his. An odd look flitted over his face, replaced by his sardonic smile so fast I couldn't be sure I'd even seen it.

"Fake boyfriend privileges." He winked and leaned in.

His tongue caught the edge of my mouth, and he licked the last of the ice cream away. A sudden fire blazed between my legs, and I couldn't hide my gasp.

Thane stiffened slightly and drew in a breath.

"Delicious." When he pulled back, he was smirking. "And the ice cream wasn't bad either."

The downside of fake dating a hellhound was definitely his ability to smell me. He knew exactly how much he was affecting my body, and it was making him cocky.

"Wait, I thought hellhounds can't eat chocolate?" I tried to play it cool and pretend my body wasn't sending the mating equivalent of smoke signals in his direction.

"I lied. We can eat just about anything," Thane purred, leaning down to kiss the tip of my nose.

I could sense there was an underlying meaning to his words, but I couldn't figure it out.

"The turmoil," I reminded both him and myself, knowing if we didn't get back on track, my self-control was going to slip, and I was going to kiss him.

"The turmoil." His expression turned serious again, and closing his fiery eyes, he took a deep breath.

He looked almost at peace like that, letting his senses drift. Something tugged on my heart. It was as though a mask had slipped from his face, and he wasn't carefully guarding every muscle movement. It reminded me of his smile when I'd given him the flowers.

"There's a lot of dust in the air. Earth. Wood splinters. I smell nothing like an explosive, so that's good. And I can't smell anyone's magical signature in the area besides yours."

"What does my magical signature smell like?" The question tumbled from my lips before I could stop it.

"Like the mountains," he replied easily. "Snowdrifts, pine, fresh air… and something else. Probably stone, but I don't have a large catalog of stony smells memorized. You don't smell like brimstone, which is a plus."

"That sounds nice," I murmured.

"It's beautiful." Thane wrapped his arm around my waist, pulling me to him.

As we walked forward, I found myself grateful for his steadying grip around me. I wasn't sure I could handle seeing the town I loved crumbled or damaged.

CHAPTER 12

VELA

To my relief, there was less damage than I'd feared. Two buildings had collapsed, and cars wouldn't be driving down the street anytime soon, but most of the town was still intact.

Was Professor Carnelian getting better? Or was it possible that it could have something to do with me?

I stepped into a puddle and growled in annoyance as cool water soaked through my shoe. Was there anything worse than soggy socks?

Glancing down, I studied the water. It was creating puddles every few feet, and it ran down the gutters to either side of the road. "Looks like a water main broke."

"I think you're right." Thane's head cocked to the side, and his eyes narrowed as though concentrating. "Hang on. I hear something."

He'd barely spoken the words before I felt it. A tiny stab of panic and fear.

We moved forward together, following our senses as they led us down the street to the corner of an old brick house. The front of the building was still standing, but the sides had fallen in, leaving a dusty, rubble-filled mess of rooms. It looked like it had been used as some sort of office.

My gargoyle magic vibrated as another stab of panic strummed it like a guitar string and this time I heard it, too. The tiniest of meows.

"It's a kitten!" I clutched Thane's arm as a swell of emotion threatened to overwhelm me. "The poor thing is terrified! We have to get it out."

The thought of the cat trapped inside that building, starving to death… No, I wouldn't let that happen.

"Let's see if we can find a safe way in." Thane moved around the corner, with me following hot on his heels.

Brick and plaster lay in a jumbled heap. A long wooden beam had fallen slantwise over the wreckage, and several interior walls were propped against each other. Thane's nostrils flared, and his eyes glowed.

"She's under those." Thane pointed to one of the fallen walls. "She must not be able to see, or else she'd have gotten out already."

My pulse jumped as the cat meowed again, and I tried to move past him.

Thane caught me around the waist, spinning me to face him. "Vela, look at me."

I tried to calm my panicked breathing and met his eyes.

His hand moved up to cup my cheek, and the familiar brush of his magic washed through me. It wove its way through my thoughts and around the emotions battering my mind and heart.

His pupils flashed to a brilliant crimson as he began draining away the emotions. I should've found his eyes eerie, but I found them calming and wondered if the intense glow was a sign of him feeding from me.

I made a mental note to ask later and focused back on the kitten who needed our help. With my emotions dampened, my mind cleared, allowing me to think rationally.

Yes, it was trapped beneath the rubble.

Yes, it needed to be rescued.

But rushing in and killing myself to save it was illogical and a waste of life. Especially when I could easily save it *without* killing myself. I was a gargoyle, which made me as strong as stone.

Sucking in a deep breath, I let my hands turn to marble. "Tell me where she is."

Thane motioned to a pile of rubble. "Under that beam. I could run back to Lycan Hall and get some extra hands to lift the beam. Otherwise, we're going to need a crane to move it."

I shook my head and stepped into the wreckage. "There are few things as strong as a gargoyle. Lifting a beam is child's play for me."

"Uh... okay. You'll need to lift it carefully so you don't bring the rest of the building down." Thane didn't sound completely convinced this would work, but I appreciated he was giving me the benefit of the doubt.

If I thought I could lift the beam, he was going to be supportive. How strange that a pretend boyfriend could be more supportive than most real boyfriends I'd observed during my time at Slaymore.

"I won't." Power surged from the ground, and knowledge of the building's weak points spread out like a map in my mind.

My feet crushed bricks and ground them to dust as I pulled part of a wall up with one hand and let it fall to the side. I slowly eased another wall up, lowering it behind me once I passed.

It was as though the old house spoke to me, telling me where to step and which spots to avoid. A reassuring calm flowed from the ground, through my body, and back into the earth.

Crouching down, I settled my shoulder under the fallen beam and lifted it inch by slow inch.

"Just a few more inches, if you can," Thane called, and I obliged.

On my knees there, in the dust, my heart ached as the frantic meowing became almost hopeful.

"We're coming, little one," I whispered into the rubble. "You're not alone."

Thane dug away chunks of drywall and broken rubble until a gray paw came into view. I carefully lifted the beam with my left shoulder and reached my hand into the mess until my fingers brushed the soft fur of a squalling gray kitten.

Like a bolt of lightning, she hooked her tiny, razor-sharp claws to my coat and shimmied up my elbow. Her blue eyes were wide as she stared straight into my face and opened her mouth to release a plaintive yowl.

Not wanting the house to collapse on top of us, I took my time lowering the beam. Thane helped me to my feet, and we picked our way back out of the building.

Once we were on steady ground, I caught the kitten in my hand and cradled her to my chest.

"Don't worry. You're safe now." I ran one finger over the kitten's head, enjoying the feel of her fur against my skin. "You're with me."

The adorable little beast began to purr. She allowed me to search her for signs of injury, and I was relieved to find she was unharmed.

Thane was looking at me oddly.

"Kitten?" I offered, gently holding her out toward him.

"My kind and cats don't really get along. Dogs and all that—" He stopped talking when the kitten looked at him and purred louder.

It was as though she had the engine of a sports car in her chest.

Thane stuck one tentative finger out for her to sniff, and I bit my lip to keep from laughing at his tense muscles and the flash of fear across his face. He fully expected to be attacked any minute.

The kitten rubbed against the offered finger, and his eyes widened with surprise before going large and soft in a way only the cutest of puppies could manage. They were the most adorable thing I'd ever laid eyes on, and I could feel my heart becoming softer than it had ever been before.

Stonehenge! I was in trouble. In a matter of days, everything I'd tried to accomplish at Slaymore had been undone. I was a failure at being a gargoyle, but when Thane's fingers tangled with mine as we petted the kitten's fur, I realized I didn't care.

I was happy.

"It seems she knows a good heart when she sees it," I said, shifting the kitten to the crook of my elbow. Going up on tiptoe, I kissed his cheek, giggling at the kiss mark my lips left in the layer of dust on his face. "She's kind of an extreme present for a first date, isn't she?"

"I never do anything halfway," he replied easily, wrapping his arm around my waist and guiding me back toward town. "I either don't bother, or I go all the way. How do you feel about dinner?"

Glancing down at my grime-covered clothing, I lifted an eyebrow. "You would take me out like this?"

"Why wouldn't I?" Thane kissed the top of my head. "I'm proud I get to take a hero to dinner. And not only are you gorgeous, you're a freaking rockstar—pun intended."

I rolled my eyes at his weird humor, but secretly, cracks in my soul that I didn't even know existed seemed to seal themselves together. Thane didn't care that I was a mess, something a gargoyle should never be.

He thought I was beautiful.

"We are only a block from the animal clinic. One of my

classmates is volunteering there, and he can cast a quick spell to make sure she doesn't have internal injuries and check for a microchip." Thane led me down the street.

It was incredible that he could be one of the paranormal world's most terrifying species and yet possess such a thoughtful heart. I wished Thane was my real boyfriend—even though, logically, I knew we couldn't have a future together.

THANE'S FRIEND determined the kitten didn't have a microchip, nor had anyone reported one missing. His friend promised to let us know if anyone came in looking for her, but it appeared as though I'd gained a cat.

I remembered one of my professors teaching a class on the magic behind the Universal Cat Distribution System. However, the mathematics had been complicated, and I'd not paid much attention as gargoyles didn't have pets, so the process didn't apply to me. Clearly, the universe had glitched and issued me my very own pint-sized house predator.

After getting a clean bill of health on the kitten, we'd left, and Thane had led me across the street and into a restaurant he claimed had the best pasta you could get in Slaymore. I watched in awe as he charmed the server into getting a bowl of cream for the kitten.

"I never really eat pasta," I confessed, straightening my silverware for the third time.

"Why not? What do gargoyles eat, rocks?" Thane teased.

"Well, actually, yeah," I admitted with a laugh. "We can eat human food, and it doesn't hurt us. Here at Slaymore, I don't eat anything with wings, mostly as a matter of principle. Gargoyles frown upon eating food for pleasure, so most of the time, we prefer minerals in their purest form."

"Sounds delicious," Thane deadpanned.

"Mineralized water can be good," I said, thinking of the fresh streams and lakes where my mother had pointed out the best sources of nutrients. "But *delicious* isn't the point."

"Well, this is going to change your mind." He slid his hand across the table and wiggled his fingers. "Fake dating privileges."

I took his offered hand and tried to ignore the heat creeping up my neck. Did he know how his touch made me want more? Is that why he took every opportunity he could for physical contact?

Clearing my throat, I tried to think of anything other than the way my heart skipped a beat every time his thumb stroked the back of my hand. "So, do they have good Italian food in the Underworld?"

Thane grinned. "Of course. Everyone comes to us eventually, including the best cooks. Hell's kitchen in the palace makes the best food in either this life or the afterlife."

His eyes softened. "I would hang out with them when I was trying to hide from my parents. The Italian chefs were the most tolerant of a kid in the kitchen but were also quick to put me to work. They had me rolling pasta, frying the perfect shrimp, and making saltimbocca when I was in elementary school."

My defective gargoyle heart ached for the lonely little boy who'd hid in the kitchen, knowing all too well what the need to escape from overbearing parents felt like. "You're just going to ease past the part where you mentioned 'hiding from your parents' by distracting me with your cooking skills?"

His fingers reflexively tightened around mine. "I don't know what else there is to say about that, really. I hid, they found me and punished me for hiding. Then the next day, they would punish me for being too loud, or running too fast, or for losing my temper, and I'd go hide again."

"That sounds…" Exhausting. Devastating. "Terrible."

"Yes, well." Thane's sarcastic smile was back, and his mask was firmly in place. "They had their perfect son, and then they had me. When I ruined my brother's life by getting bonded to *his* princess, my family despised me even more."

"Is that why you're here? At Slaymore, I mean?"

He nodded. "Yeah. I couldn't do anything right in their eyes. Bonding to the princess was just one of my failures. When a hellhound feeds, that feeding should last for a while. But thanks to my erratic emotions, I burn through feedings far too fast and need to feed again. That wouldn't be so bad if I could enhance emotions in a person before I feed from them, but I can't even do that. Which makes me an inconvenience that neither my family nor the royal family wanted to deal with."

I did what a gargoyle did best. Remaining silent, I let him talk as I listened.

"The last straw was when I lost control and drained all emotions from the perv propositioning the princess. My stuff was packed, and I was brought to Slaymore. I told them I'd make something of myself and make them proud."

And did you? I wanted to ask but didn't.

I had a feeling I knew the answer. And indeed, Thane didn't need me to ask.

He could see the question in my eyes. "They didn't care what I did as long as I wasn't around. They haven't been here once in the last three and a half years. And the longer I'm here, the more I question why I care so much when I know how little I mean to them."

"Even your brother?" I had no siblings, but all my room-mates did.

At least once a year, their families arrived at Slaymore, full of shrieking, hugging, grumbling, and bickering. They had seemed close to their families.

"He's too busy studying. We're both studying business since hellhounds are more than just bodyguards for the royal family of Hades; we're also advisers. When I officially take up my post, I'll have a hand in some of the biggest business decisions of the Underworld."

"So that's your future. A businessman." Somehow, Thane didn't strike me as the type.

Thane spread his arms and sighed. "Alas, it is my fate."

We paused as the waiter brought some wine. "Compliments of the chef," he said, pouring a fruity-smelling white into two glasses.

Thane closed his eyes as he took an appreciative sniff.

"Tell Brenzino he's a star," he said with one of those rare, real smiles.

As the waiter left, I asked, "What do you *really* want to do with yourself?"

Thane picked up his wineglass and shrugged. "Does it matter?"

"Of course it matters." Although even as I said it, I wasn't sure.

My fate had been decided for me before my conception had been contracted. I was bound to it no matter what I wanted.

But I truly do want to be the guardian of a city, I reminded myself. So my situation was different.

"I'd like to be my brother," Thane joked, but a deep orange flicker of resentment flashed in his eyes.

"Be serious." I leaned forward, tightening my fingers on him on purpose. "You're not your twin, and you can never be. You can just be you. So who is that?"

"I never mentioned that my brother was my twin. Have you been spying on me, little gargoyle?"

I took a long drink from my glass before admitting, "We arrived at Slaymore on the same day. I might have noticed you and your family."

"I know." Thane's eyes sparkled with amusement. "Because I watched you too."

"You did?" My voice squeaked, and my heart melted a little, knowing he'd noticed me.

"You're hard to miss with that mane of lilac hair." A beautiful smile flashed across his face, then dimmed. "And you looked just as miserable as I felt, although you were doing better at hiding it."

I didn't know what to say and remained silent.

"You asked me who I was." He sighed, tapping his finger on the table next to his wineglass. "I like art. Professor Carnelian used to give me painting assignments as a way to express and incite emotion in myself. He thought it might help to explore my emotions along with my powers. He always told me there was a link between the way my magic misfired and the way I learned to push down my own emotions as a kid."

"He wanted you to be... more emotional? The gargoyle professor?" I could barely contain my confusion.

Gargoyles despised art for the very reason that it stirred unnecessary and messy emotions. I couldn't imagine any self-respecting gargoyle encouraging someone to indulge in the arts.

"Carnelian told me he learned long ago not to hold his feelings in contempt." Thane was looking at me as though it were my turn to learn something. "He held them dear, he examined them, and then he used them as the basis for his logic. While he didn't express the emotions, he always had them."

I looked down at the table. Neither my parents nor any members of the gargoyle Council I'd met had admitted to having emotions. I was taught that a gargoyle might express emotions as a baby, but they learned to turn them off before they even learned to shift forms.

The pasta came, halting our conversation, and Thane gave my hand a brief squeeze before letting it go.

I took a taste of my shrimp *fra diavolo*. It was spicy, and the shrimp was... well, shrimp. I didn't think I'd know the difference between good shrimp and bad unless I got food poisoning.

"What do you think?" Thane asked, sipping his wine.

"It's all right," I said, feeling a little defensive. "I mean, gargoyles aren't really connoisseurs of human food, so I don't have a great palate."

Thane surprised me by laughing. "You won't insult me if you don't like the food, Vela. I said it's the best in Slaymore. It's not the best ever. Besides, everyone has the right to an opinion on Italian food." He paused to enjoy a bite of his lasagna. "Even if your opinions are wrong." He shot me a playful wink.

I tried to scowl but ruined it by giggling. "Who knew hellhounds could be so judgmental?"

He shrugged. "It's part of the job."

The pasta *was* fine, and the wine was better. I let Thane pour me a second glass, though I took it slow. We had a mystery to solve and classes to get to tomorrow; it wouldn't do to be hungover.

We'd finished our plates and were arguing over the merits of dessert when I heard a tapping at the window. A raven hopped on the ledge, twisting its head this way and that. My new kitten friend hissed from her place in my lap, tail lashing.

"I think I need to take this." Scooping her up, I handed her to Thane and hurried outside.

I pretended to shoo the raven around the side of the building. The moment we were out of eyesight, I crouched in the alley and stuck out my hand.

"All right, what's wrong?"

He hopped onto my fingers and let out a caw. With the physical contact, images bloomed before my mind's eye. Carnelian's bed, soaked with strange fluids. The professor, thrashing. The monitor linked to his heart, letting out a long, angry wail. Nurses rushing in.

I let him give me the whole story before heading back inside. The lightness I'd felt at dinner was gone, replaced by sorrow and shame. Here I was, flirting with a hellhound while Professor Carnelian was on his deathbed and Slaymore was in crisis.

Thane took one look at my face and stood. "What's wrong?"

Collapsing heavily onto the seat, I leaned over the table. "Professor Carnelian's worse." A lump formed in my throat.

"That's awful." Thane put his hand on my wrist. "I'm guessing he was a father figure to you, too."

His presence was reassuring, and I was glad he didn't spout some useless platitudes about how everything would turn out fine.

"He understood me." Part of me didn't know why I was telling him the truth. "More than any gargoyle ever has. He was the first person who didn't treat me like I was defective."

A tear slid down my cheek, and I angrily dashed it away. "I just—I love Slaymore so much, and I care about him, and the more I care, the worse things seem to get, and I can't let all this emotion cloud my mind…"

The ground rumbled beneath us as though answering me. The wineglasses in the restaurant clanged against each other like wind chimes on their racks, and the tables rocked. Our server grabbed the edge of the wall, eyes wide.

"It's happening again." Thane paled, and in his arms, the kitten hissed.

"We need to get out of here." I needed to fly Thane out of here before he got hurt.

I leaped to my feet and spun to grab Thane's hand, only to stop dead in my tracks as I looked outside.

The last people I'd ever expected to see in Slaymore town were staring back at me through the window. And even though gargoyles expressed no emotion, I could feel the disapproval radiating from them through the glass.

My parents.

CHAPTER 13

VELA

My father opened the door, allowing my mother to walk inside first before he ducked his head and stepped in behind her. They were using illusion spells to hide their wings, but there was no hiding my father's impressive height.

Mother's businesslike heels clicked on the tile floor as she entered, waving off the server as he came forward to greet them. She wore a mourning suit comprising a black jacket, skirt, and tie. Even her shirt was black. Her hair was pulled into a bun so severe I was surprised it didn't warp the skin of her face.

"Vela, what is this?" She gestured at the table, the kitten, and Thane. "And what are you wearing?" Her eyes took in my mud-covered tights and the low-cut green dress Meri had given me.

For a wild, rebellious moment, I considered giving her a heart attack by telling her Thane was my boyfriend, but then I thought of how she would likely react, and I knew that removing me from Slaymore that same night would be the gentlest outcome.

It was more likely she and Father would conclude I was a lost cause, turn me to stone, and give me a hundred years to dwell on my many shortcomings.

Thane shifted to stand behind me. The back of my dress had an intricate braided design that exposed small bits of my skin, and he used that to brush his fingers against my spine. My nerves spiked at that simplest of touches, then, just as quickly, they faded.

Like a good little gargoyle, my voice went flat, and my face became smooth and cold as marble. Slate! My gargoyle form was more expressive than the mask I wore at that moment.

"This is my business associate, Thane. He and I are investigating the odd events that have occurred in Slaymore town over the past two days. As for my dress, you will find that it is the prevailing style of Slaymore town, which has a number of mundane citizens and requires certain cessions if one wishes to blend in. Thane, this is Corata and Falkor. Their bodies gave me life." I arched an eyebrow toward the pair who towered over me. "Though it does little to explain why you are here."

Corata nodded, accepting the logic of my explanation. "The Council received an unwelcome message from Headmistress Losia. She tells us that your Professor Carnelian is dying?"

My pain, which had been gut-wrenching fifteen minutes before, was only a distant stab in my heart, thanks to Thane's fingers against my skin. "We were aware that he is ill, though not the extent of it."

"The headmistress is not qualified to perform embalming and funerary rites on gargoyles. The Council felt it was best to send representatives. As we were due to check in on your progress, we felt it logical that we attend to the matter."

I cooly tilted my chin in acknowledgment. "I see."

"I don't see." Thane stepped away from me.

He was still clutching the kitten, holding her protectively against his chest. His cheeks looked rosy and full, and his eyes flashed with life... and barely contained anger. "Are you telling me Carnelian's *dying*?"

"The current signs indicate the end of his natural life is imminent," Corata answered without a fleck of sympathy.

Thane's mouth grew thin as he turned to me. "Vela, I don't understand. I thought you said he was worse. You didn't say he was dying."

I shook my head. "I had to extrapolate from what the raven understood. I did not take the images to mean he was dying."

Corata's hard-as-steel gaze looked Thane up and down. "Pardon the question, but why are you here? What is your attachment to Professor Carnelian?" She looked back and forth between us. "Or my daughter?"

Just a few minutes ago, that question would have sent me into a spiral of panic. Without my tumultuous emotions, I could stand calmly and let Thane speak for himself.

"What, so only gargoyles can care about other gargoyles?" he said sarcastically. "Carnelian was my mentor, too. I don't want him to die."

"Care is irrelevant. Death comes to all." Corata looked at him as though he were highly illogical and a waste of her time.

"Because of his emotional attachment, Thane wished to investigate this matter together," I said before Thane could let loose with a string of profanities. "We believe Professor Carnelian's condition is related to certain happenings in town."

"That is valuable information to have. Thank you," Falkor said, speaking for the first time. He leveled his deep purple eyes on me. "You are not being ruled by emotion, and it seems you have improved greatly in your years studying here. We will report your progress to the Council."

"Thank you." I bowed my head slightly as gargoyle custom dictated.

Spinning on their heel, they turned and left without so much as a goodbye.

"Our meal is over, so we should go as well," I said. "Please allow me to pay. I know you're angry."

"I already paid when you were out communing with your crow," Thane bit out.

He grabbed his jacket and put it on with one hand, holding the kitten the whole time.

"Raven. But I understand it is not always easy to see the difference," I corrected.

We left the restaurant and headed back toward the academy. The moon had risen, casting her silver glow over the town. The air smelled sharp and salty, and I felt a pang of longing, though it was distant and muffled by Thane's magic.

"You're angry with me," I said as we walked.

Thane puffed out a breath. "Yeah. Carnelian's *dying*, and you just… stand around like a robot? It's like someone told you it was going to rain tomorrow, not that we were about to lose someone we care about."

"What can I do about it?" I was truthfully curious. Sticking my hands in the pockets of my coat, I studied his profile.

"You can be mad about it. You can be sad about it. You can be *something*." He shoved his hair out of his face, and I saw the jerk of muscles in his jaw.

The glow of his pupils was more red than orange, a sign I was coming to associate with anger—or desire. The latter didn't seem likely.

"You removed my ability to feel those things," I pointed out.

Thane kicked a loose stone and sent it skittering down the road. "Yeah, I know. So I'm also angry with myself."

"Why? It was useful, and it assisted us in keeping our cover. When I can feel again, I will be grateful."

"But that's exactly what I'm trying *not* to do. I almost went too far when I drained you. My mentor's dying, and now it feels like he wasted the last three years of his life. I can't fail him. I can't fail at this."

The kitten stretched, her tiny claws picking holes in his coat. Thane stroked her back, unconcerned about the damage. This was why pets were illogical. They created messes and caused damages that could be avoided by not owning them.

"It's not failure, if it's what you were trying to do," I said.

We came to the edge of town and slipped through the magical barrier. My wings snapped open in reflex, stretching out and fluttering in the night air. I felt a whisper of relief at them being freed.

"It was too easy. I didn't even think about it." Thane's shoulders hunched forward. "And I don't like you like this. You're full of life, curiosity, and passion… I hate seeing you constantly trying to stifle that, and now I'm the one responsible for it."

I had nothing productive to add to the conversation, so I remained silent. When we reached the path that led toward the student housing, I expected him to split off and leave me alone.

But Thane remained at my side, walking me all the way to the front door. It was pleasant to share the silence with someone, even if his silence was a brooding one. As I set my mind to thinking about what he said, a potential solution formed in my mind.

I stopped in front of my house. "You fear you can still

take emotion, but you can't give it." It was a statement, not a question.

"Yeah. And if I can't make people feel heightened fear, then I can't perform the job I was born and raised to do." He didn't say it, but we both knew that would mean he'd continue to be a failure in his and his parents' eyes.

"The logical solution would be to see if you can incite the emotions in me that you took away. Reverse the process, so to speak." I cocked my head, watching as moonlight washed over his face, sharpening the curve of his cheekbone and the slant of his nose.

Even in my current bland state, I could see he was beautiful and statuesque. "Experimenting on a gargoyle might be more difficult, but the potential payoff is greater," I added.

"Tell me about it." Thane shook his head. "Until I met your parents, I underestimated how stone-cold gargoyles could be. I can't enhance emotions in species that have abundant emotions. There isn't a chance I can enhance them in a species with nonexistent emotions."

"So you must incite or instill them in me, and then you can enhance," I told him flatly. "Previously, you have incited anger, gratitude, and lust within me. Most recently gratitude, but most strongly lust."

"Well, this conversation has taken a strange turn." He looked at the kitten, who mewled up at him as though wanting to add her input. Thane lifted his gaze, a small smirk playing at the corners of his mouth. "Or is that flirty gargoyle speak for asking me to kiss you again?"

"I'm incapable of successfully flirting on my worst days as a gargoyle. That can't have improved now that I feel no desire or lust."

Thane's laugh was harsh, lacking any real amusement.

Tilting my head, I considered him. "It will be a challenge, but this is the most efficient way for you to practice your abilities and test your skills."

He stepped closer. "So it's strictly scientific."

If I'd still had my emotions, I would have been flushing at his nearness. But I was currently doing the best impression of a proper gargoyle I'd ever managed.

"Okay." Thane seemed to be speaking more to himself than anyone else. "Okay. I can do this."

He closed the gap between us. Putting his free hand on my arm, he leaned in.

This kiss wasn't like the first. He started more tentatively, brushing his lips gently against mine as if he feared I'd push him away.

Wanting to encourage him in this experiment, I slipped my hand around his neck. It worked, and he grew bolder. He kissed me again, taking my bottom lip between his teeth and sucking gently.

A tiny spark stirred in the recesses of my consciousness. Not the emotion itself, but the desire to feel something... *anything*.

I knew if I reached out, I'd be able to grasp that desire and experience all the things normal people felt when they kissed. The emotions I'd experienced when he'd kissed me the first time.

So, I reached out.

And everything flooded back with a vengeance.

Fire licked over my entire body, and my mouth opened in a moan. Thane tangled his tongue with mine, and I cupped the back of his head to pull him closer.

I leaned into him, desperately trying to fit our bodies together to find that spot that would soothe the ache between my legs. Or maybe I was hoping to inflame it.

He swallowed my whimpers as the need to feel his hands on every part of me intensified with each gasping breath I took. I longed to feel his hands brushing over my skin in places that no one else had ever touched. More than anything, I wanted to know what it would be like to feel my bare skin against his with nothing separating us.

But behind the desire came more emotion. Emotions I'd been on the brink of feeling when my parents had inter-rupted us.

Tears filled my eyes and spilled down my cheeks. My gasps of desire turned to choking sobs.

Thane pulled away. "Whoa, *whoa*." He cupped my cheek, his eyes filled with concern as they searched mine. "You should have told me to stop. Did I hurt you?"

"No," I hiccuped. My voice squeaked as I fought to speak without breaking down. "I just... don't want to lose him. He was a better father than my own father."

I buried my face in Thane's shirt and sobbed.

"*Meow*," said the kitten plaintively, kneading her paws in my mess of purple hair.

It was enough to break the spell. I couldn't help but

laugh as I turned to look at the kitten. She still sat in the crook of Thane's arm, eyeing me balefully.

"I'm sorry." I tried to pull away, but Thane slipped his arm around me. He held me pressed into him, not caring that I was soaking his shirt. "I wouldn't normally cry like this. But you…"

"Enhanced?" He sounded hopeful.

"Enhanced *everything.* I'm still so upset about Carnelian, and I can't believe my parents are here. It's all too much to handle at once." I palmed my eyes. "But I really was enjoying it—"

"I know." His voice turned sly. "I could smell you."

I laughed again, this time in a mixture of relief and embarrassment. "That's the worst. I can't believe—"

"Beautiful girl, it is far from the worst." Thane buried his nose in my neck and breathed deeply. Every hair on my body stood on end, and I arched against him.

"It's…" he groaned. "It's sexy as Hades. And I should know since I've been there. I want you to express your desire, and not just because it would mean success."

"Well," I cleared my throat, "we're focusing on you and your powers, so let's forget about me for a second."

An odd expression crossed Thane's face, as though he'd just tasted something gross. "No. I'm not going to forget about you. Not ever."

His finger ran down my coat, undoing the buttons and brushing against the edge of my low-cut dress. Goosebumps rose in the wake of his touch.

I wanted to kiss him again. Badly.

Actually, forget kissing. I longed to do so much more.

For the first time in my life, I wondered what sex was like.

What would it be like between two people who cared about each other and ached for each other? Rather than a contractual obligation.

It was as though he could read my mind.

"What do you want?" he whispered.

"*Meow*," the kitten mumbled between us.

We laughed again, our hearts a little lighter.

"I want to go inside before my parents catch us. And we need to get that thing somewhere warm and dry, with lots of milk and good food." I barely stopped myself from adding *a place where she can be distracted while we... entertain ourselves.*

"I'd like to see you paint," I blurted.

At first, I didn't know where that had come from, but as soon as I said it, I knew it was true. It was a part of Thane that was personal, beyond physical.

He arched an eyebrow, and I thought he was going to argue with me. Then, that sly spark of embers I was growing to love glowed in his eyes again.

"I have an idea," he said.

CHAPTER 14

VELA

Thane had left me to make a trip to his dorm. He promised to be back in a handful of minutes, so I decided to use the time to get the kitten settled in.

The door was unlocked, so tucking the cat inside my coat, I stepped into the kitchen. Meg was at the sink washing dishes but turned when she heard the squeak of the door opening.

Her eyes widened as she took me in. "What happened?"

I realized I was still smeared with mud and grime. My eyes were probably red from my bursting-into-tears moment, too. "It's been a long day. Um…"

Then her eyes landed on the furball, who popped her head from inside my coat to peer around the kitchen. "Is that a *cat?*"

I scratched the kitten behind her ears. "Do you think we could keep her?"

Meg dried her hands on a towel and rushed forward, pushing her round glasses up her button nose.

Her eyes were already sparkling, even as she said, "Meri's never said yes to any pet. Ever."

"That was when it was all theoretical. Now it's real. And besides, I found her in a collapsed building. It's not like she has a home to go back to." I cuddled the kitten, my stomach twisting at the image of turning her out to the elements.

Then I had a better idea and held her out to Meg.

Meg scooped her gently into her arms and nuzzled her nose to nose.

"You are sweet," she cooed. "You *are*. What's your name, cutie?"

She looked up at me expectantly.

"Uh..."

"You didn't even name her? She's got to be called something. It'll make it harder for Meri to say no." Meg held her up to the light, and the kitten played her part by meowing piteously. "Silver's too on the nose, I think."

She looked at me again. It was clearly a prompt for me to say something. "Well, we found her in the rubble..."

"Absolutely not. You can't call her Rubble." Meg rolled her eyes.

"Granite?" I suggested, running a finger along the kitten's ear. Though, now that I thought about it, her gray coloring might be from the dirt and dust.

There was a soft knock, and the door opened again.

Thane reappeared, hair windblown and cheeks reddened from the wind.

He set a canvas bag on the floor to slip off his coat. He'd changed into something less filthy. I watched with interest as his red tee slid up, showing the curve of his hip as he hung his coat on the coat rack.

Meg's mouth fell open.

Bending, he picked up his bag and grinned at us. For a moment, I forgot how to speak. "What are you two talking about? Did I miss anything fun?"

It took my brain a few moments to process what he'd said. "We were trying to name the kitten," I managed, looking to Meg for support.

She was still staring.

"That's easy. Her name's Sapphire. For her eyes." Thane reached out to scratch under her chin.

Sapphire blinked her deep blue eyes and purred.

Then he looked at Meg. "Do you think Sapphire could hang out with you for a little while? We have a, uh, painting project."

Meg finally closed her mouth and swallowed.

"No problem," she managed in a strangled voice.

"Great." Thane's smile warmed his voice, and his hand slipped into mine, pulling me toward the stairs.

A full body flush traveled from the roots of my hair all the way down to my toes.

I cast a glance back over my shoulder at Meg, whose eyes were shining.

Get it, girl, she mouthed and winked.

Thane and I went up the stairs hand in hand. "Which one's yours? No, let me guess."

Thane paused, taking in a deep breath, then turned to the right. He walked up to the second door down the hall and arched an eyebrow at me.

"Correct," I said.

He pushed open the door.

"Cozy," he remarked, and I couldn't tell if he was being sarcastic or not.

I sat on the bed as he put the canvas bag down on my desk. He took out pot after tiny pot of pigment in every shade of the rainbow.

"No canvas?" I said. "I don't have any paper. Not any nice paper, anyway."

"You're the canvas." He darted a sly look at me. "This is face paint. I want to try painting my emotions on someone else's face. Usually, it's my own face I paint, so having a model will be nice."

"I've never had my face painted before." I crossed my legs and settled my skirt over my lap.

"Never?" His eyebrows rose. "Not even at the funfair or some festival or something?"

I snorted. "Do you seriously think gargoyles go to funfairs?"

"Good point." Thane chuckled, though his eyes flashed with sadness.

He finished setting up his pigments and laid out an array of paintbrushes. Some were as thick as my thumb, others had only a few strands of hair.

He borrowed my tea mug from my night table and filled it with water from the bathroom sink.

Coming back into the room, he shut the door. "We need some music. What do you listen to?"

"Mostly city noises, I guess."

Gargoyles held little regard for music. Our music was the symphony of the world, of people fighting, singing, and laughing together. Of rain on a roof or against a windowpane. Of cars honking and birds singing.

"Oh, right." Thane drew out his phone and found a playlist. "Lo-Fi. No distractions. Just a few nice beats."

He kneeled in front of me and looked up, orange eyes sparking with red. I'd never realized how long his lashes were before. Before I could think better of it, I leaned in and gave him a soft kiss, enjoying the way he smiled against my mouth.

When I pulled away, he held up the brush. "All right. What do you want?"

"Whatever you think is best." I shrugged. "You're the artist, after all."

He cocked his head, catching my chin between his fingers and turning my head this way and that as he studied my face. Then he nodded and picked up a little jar of blue paint.

The first swipe on my face felt like cool raindrops streaking down my cheek, though as it dried, it felt more like mud on my skin.

I wrinkled my nose. "That feels... odd."

"Shh. I'm just warming up." Thane's breath tickled my ear.

His eyes narrowed, and his eyebrows drew together in concentration.

The warmth radiating from his body distracted me from the tickle of the paintbrush against my skin. Heat poured from him, so strong I was surprised I'd never noticed it before.

Thane's arms moved in elegant, precise lines as he painted, showing off the line of his collarbone where it disappeared under his tee. His silky hair kept falling over his eyes, and he would periodically toss his head to the side to get rid of them.

Reaching up, I tucked a strand of his dark hair behind one ear. The lopsided smile he gave me had my heart tripping over its beat, and I wondered if he could hear it.

The paintbrush swiped along my jaw, causing me to inhale sharply at the sensual sensation.

Thane paused. "Was that a good gasp or a bad gasp?"

"Good, I think," I replied, a little breathless.

"Better make sure," he leaned in and stroked the paintbrush along my jaw a second time.

I gasped again, and my wings twitched without my permission. It tickled but in a good way.

Thane lowered the paintbrush and placed his mouth against my neck. His lips were searing and sent desire shivering down my body. My wings snapped open.

"This is new," Thane murmured, running a finger along

the top of one leathery wing. Fire seemed to follow in his wake.

"They're... sensitive," I managed.

Although, they weren't usually *this* sensitive. I guess when you lay with hellhounds, everything gets heightened. Not that I was complaining.

"I noticed." A wicked smile slid across his face, promising naughtiness was to come.

He lifted his paintbrush again and stroked it along the membrane that connects the bones. All coherent thoughts fled my body, and I went limp against my bed.

Thane leaned over me, continuing to paint my skin and trail desire from one end of me to the other. Fire pooled between my legs and radiated outward until everything in me tingled, and every touch made my breath catch.

With every hitch of my breath, his eyes burned hotter, and the paintbrush strokes grew bolder. It dipped along the neckline of my dress and teased its way up my thigh. My nipples hardened under my bra, and I grew unbearably hot.

I sat up suddenly, snapping my wings shut against my back. Thane jerked back to avoid being knocked off the bed.

His hooded, lustful expression was replaced by one of concern. "What's wrong?"

Nothing was wrong. Not giving myself a chance to second-guess it, I stood, yanking the green dress over my head and letting it flutter to the floor. Then I unhooked my bra.

Thane's hungry gaze devoured my exposed skin. His

bottom lip caught between his teeth, and fire flickered in his eyes.

Moving to stand in front of him, I grabbed the edge of his shirt. As I pulled it off him, he seemed to come back to himself. Thane stood, fumbling with his belt and letting his jeans fall to the floor.

Then we were standing there, me in my underwear and him in his boxers. His cock strained against the fabric, and I remembered the rock-hard bulge that had pressed against my belly in the closet.

Suddenly, I couldn't think of anything but how it might feel between my fingers… or, better yet, between my legs.

He moved toward me, and we tumbled back onto the bed in a tangle of limbs. His mouth found my neck, and his hands stroked down my ribs, fluttered over my hips, and tugged at the edge of my panties.

When his thumb found a nipple and rolled it gently back and forth, I bucked my hips in response. The movement caused me to grind against the hardness in his boxers, and Thane's growl vibrated through me.

My desire doubled.

I could do little more than cling to him as he ran his tongue along my jaw, then worked downward, leaving a trail of kisses from my neck to one nipple and then the other. His tongue curled around one hardened peak before he sucked it into his mouth.

"Oh, Thane," I moaned, wriggling beneath him as he continued to kiss his way to my belly button.

He paused at the top of my underwear to give me a

questioning look. "Should we stop?" the sexy hellhound asked softly.

"I will absolutely *murder* you if you stop," I snarled, my voice as hard as granite.

In response, he took my underwear in his teeth and pulled. He eased it over my knees, then ran his hands back up my thighs. His mouth followed, searing my skin each time his hot lips pressed against me.

As his kisses moved higher, my legs quivered, earning a husky chuckle from Thane. My body grew more demanding, sending wave after wave of slick heat rushing between my thighs. He stopped mere centimeters from my aching core, and I was equal parts turned on and embarrassed when his eyes closed and he breathed my scent deep into his lungs.

Then his eyes snapped open, and with excruciating slowness, his tongue lapped along my slit. My hips bucked off the bed without my permission, and I whimpered.

Thane's long fingers curled around my hips, holding me in place as his tongue delved inside me. That first hard thrust had me forgetting anything else existed.

Pleasure built upon pleasure, heightening inside me before being devoured by Thane… only to circle back to me until I couldn't contain myself anymore.

His tongue grew thicker and longer, and even with my eyes closed, I knew he must have shifted his tongue. It was a reminder that he was more than just a cute guy, and for a second, I questioned my sanity in bringing a hellhound into my bed. Maybe I should have started with something less, well, dangerous.

No, he was the only guy I'd ever wanted to be touched by.

And deep in my soul, I knew I'd never allow another guy to touch me so intimately. He was the only one for me.

Thane's tongue plunged deeper, stroking places inside me I didn't know existed. I gave a startled cry, looking at him with panic as wave after wave of pleasure crashed through me.

I had no way of knowing what to expect, and it was more than my mind or body could process. My breathing was coming in sharp gasps, and my body trembled. It was incredible, overwhelming, and terrifying all at once.

Thane crawled up to loom over me, his arms braced on either side. He pressed his forehead into mine. "You're safe. Relax and enjoy it. I swear, you're safe."

And so I closed my eyes and rode out the waves of pleasure.

"I'm not sure I'll ever walk again," I confessed when I could finally speak again. In truth, I could barely feel anything below my waist.

"No higher praise than that." He smirked, moving to lie next to me, pressing his back to the wall and holding me tight against his chest.

I could feel the burning length of his cock against my thigh. "Do you, um, want me to return the favor?"

Thane chuckled. "Believe me, you did me the favor. I don't want you to do anything unless you want to." He put his head back, eyelids fluttering closed. "But just so you know, you can do anything you want to me."

Biting my lip, I made my decision. Hooking one finger inside his boxers, I pulled them down until his cock sprang free.

I'd seen penises in anatomy classes, and I understood the basics of copulation. After all, it was only logical to understand what went where so no valuable time was wasted during copulation.

Likewise, gargoyles didn't waste time learning or teaching about how to give their partner pleasure since that had nothing to do with successful mating.

I'd had to learn what a clitoris was from Meri. Basically, anything I knew about how other species performed sex came from Meri, with her loud mouth and no filter. She loved to tell the tales of her escapades over breakfast the morning after.

Leaning over, I lightly kissed the tip of his length. It jerked against my hand in response. I darted my tongue along his length, and Thane gasped. Emboldened, I slipped my lips over the head and sucked him deep into my mouth.

"Vela," he growled.

I took my time exploring him, experimenting with my tongue, lips, and fingers. Thane tangled a hand in my hair, guiding me gently but never pushing.

His cock pulsed in my mouth, which in turn made my desire grow. And the more he groaned, the wetter I grew between my legs.

At last, he shuddered, his muscles growing stiff. Curious, I pulled away, watching in amazement as he came apart in my hand.

He grabbed a towel covered in dried paint and wiped me clean. When he finished, he snaked an arm around my waist and pulled me down to him.

"You're glorious," he murmured. "Absolutely incredible."

"Yeah?" I snuggled closer and tilted my chin up to meet his eyes. "Because I want you again."

"Really?" Embers popped and sparked in his glowing eyes.

"It's the truth." I was a gargoyle, and I wanted him more than I'd ever wanted anything. "Logic and logical copulation can take a trip straight to Hades."

I wanted to feel complete, and I wanted to feel that with Thane... as many times as I could.

Thane chuckled and let his head flop back on my pillow. "Give me five minutes," he said. "Then I'll be ready to rock your world. Over and over."

CHAPTER
15

VELA

We slept until almost noon. Which made sense, considering the sky had already begun lightening by the time Thane had emerged from between my legs for the final time. He'd flopped on top of me, pulled the sheet around us, and we'd drifted off in a sticky, blissful sleep.

"Breakfast," I declared as I woke. My stomach rumbled in agreement.

Thane propped himself up on one of his elbows. His eyes were dulled by sleep, and his hair hid half his face. How was he so beautiful?

"Huh." He squinted at my clock. "I missed class."

I sat up abruptly. "Sorry! Maybe if we get you dressed, we can—"

But Thane laughed and nuzzled my neck. "Don't

worry about it. I'm getting a C in that class anyway, and I'm not going to do any better by rushing in to make the last five minutes. Let's just enjoy breakfast together."

I told Thane he could take a shower first, but he pulled me into the bathroom after him and gave me a delicious rub down with the soap. By the time he finished, I was ready to drag him back to bed. But our growling bellies drew us downstairs instead...

Where we found all my roommates sitting around the dining table.

"Welcome." Meri leaned back and took a sip of her mimosa. "Brunch?"

She knew *exactly* what I'd been doing last night, and she didn't bother to hide her grin.

I longed to crawl under the table and die, but Thane took a seat and pulled me into the chair next to him. "Thanks for the invitation."

Kaya had been on a baking streak, so we helped ourselves to cinnamon rolls and homemade bread. Meg had scrambled some eggs, so I made myself a towering egg sandwich with avocado covered in hot sauce.

I kept my mouth full, partly because of hunger but also because I needed to avoid talking to my roommates ever again. Thankfully, the introductions had gone around the table without me saying a peep.

As Kaya poured Thane equal parts orange juice and sparkling wine, she asked, "So what do you do?"

Thane smiled. "I study. What do *you* do?"

"Law," Kaya said with a sunny smile. "As soon as we graduate, anyway."

"Right. Well, I'm a contracted hellhound, so my future's pretty much been set since I was six."

While Thane talked to them about the intricacies of life in the Underworld, I snuck glances around the table. Meg had little Sapphire in her lap, feeding her bits of cheese.

Meri was smiling broadly as she listened to Thane, though when she caught my eye, she winked. Kaya asked him a few questions, mostly contract-related, as she nibbled on her cinnamon roll.

"So you can't void or otherwise end your contract?" she asked when he paused to finish his eggs.

"Contracts signed in Hades have a reputation for being pretty soul-binding and impossible to break." Thane's smile turned from polite to sardonic as he lowered his mimosa glass. "The guardianship of Princess Eliana was always intended for my brother. But when a connection is forged, it's forged forever."

Kaya cleared her throat. "You don't seem so happy about that."

Thane lifted one shoulder. "And what has happiness to do with life and responsibilities?"

"I'm sorry for all the questions. This is just an area of interest for me," Kaya said.

Thane waved away her apology.

"I'm interested in contract law among paranormals, and I think that in many cases, outdated traditions have resulted in unfair binding contracts. It's something I want to work with when I'm interning with Vitaly." Kaya's eyes sparkled as she finished.

"Vitaly and Sons?" Thane raised his eyebrows. "Even I've heard of them."

The conversation turned to other things as Meri started whining about a paper she had to write this weekend.

As they spoke, I noticed Thane was picking at his food. After breakfast, he pushed back from the table.

"I'd better go apologize to Professor Mackenzie," he said. "And grab some make-up homework."

I nodded. "Good luck."

"Yeah." He leaned forward toward me, and I thought he was going to kiss me. But something passed across his face, and he cleared his throat. "Let's, um, think about our next move regarding Professor Carnelian. Maybe find out how bad things really are."

"Okay," I whispered, trying to hide the disappointment at his sudden coolness from my voice.

He pulled his coat on and let the door slam behind him… without looking back.

Something was definitely bothering him, but I couldn't quite put my finger on it. Before I had the chance to really think it through, Meri slung her arm around me, pulling me close and crushing my side to hers.

I squawked in surprise.

"Girl, you *got* it. You finally got your rocks off, and I couldn't be prouder!" Her enormous hand came up in front of my face. "High five."

I squirmed out of her grip.

For the first time in my life, I was eager to go full-on gargoyle.

"I'd prefer not to discuss my private life in such terms," I said as primly as I could.

Meri just laughed. "Vela, we heard your private life all night last night. You've now taken part in a very important Slaymore tradition—sex with a hot boy in a bed far too small. Now it's time for another tradition: dishing with your friends."

I wanted to melt into a puddle. Instead, I tried to flee up the stairs. It was futile because Meri caught me easily and frog-marched me back to the kitchen.

"If you heard everything, then there's nothing to tell," I protested, trying to figure out if I could hide with Sapphire under the table.

"Nope, you owe me. You brought a furball into my house last night, and if you want the little creature to stay, you're going to talk. What's Thane like?"

Sapphire purred, weaving between Meri's legs.

"Not now. I'm trying to seem intimidating." Meri eyed the kitten, then added in a stage whisper, "We'll cuddle later."

"He seems nice," Meg started.

"But potentially problematic." Kaya put her chin in her hands. "Is this a long-term thing? Because if he's contracted to a princess of Hades, he can't exactly stay with you in your city when you become a guardian."

Meri rolled her eyes. "Maybe he's just a fling. Vela doesn't have to settle down with the first pogo-stick she hops on. Let a girl have fun, Kaya."

"There was no pogo-stick riding happening last night!" I huffed.

Meri's jaw dropped. "Hang on. You were making all that racket, and the man was only using only his mouth? Maybe I need to find myself a hellhound."

"I don't know what he is… what we are," I answered Kaya, trying to steer away from revealing any more about what had happened the night before.

That wasn't exactly true, though. I wanted Thane for as long as he was willing to be with me.

Rubbing my forehead, I added, "I don't know what he wants, either. We haven't really talked about it."

"What do you want this thing between you to be?" Meg asked softly.

"Gargoyles—" I began.

"*Boring.*" Meri smacked me lightly on the back.

She propped her feet up on Thane's chair, then grabbed the orange juice and sloshed some into her glass. "Gargoyles can want because we can all see that you have hopes and desires. And I don't care what your hard-headed council says, you are a freaking amazing gargoyle. You want the demon doggo, and it's okay to talk about it."

"She's right." Kaya reached out to squeeze my hand.

I looked from face to face. Three good friends, maybe the best of friends, were trying to help me. When had they ever steered me wrong? Other than when they'd told me coffee tasted good.

They had good and caring hearts. Unlike my mother

and father, they'd listened to me. They'd see my emotions as a part of what made me who I was rather than some defect that needed to be cut away.

"I want… I think I want to be with Thane. To see what a real relationship is all about."

I WAITED for Thane to text that he was done with class, but he never did. Trying to pretend it didn't bother me, I stopped by the healing wing to ask about Professor Carnelian's current condition, but the same tough-as-nails nurse shooed me right back out the door.

The next few hours were spent in classes. Then I spent a listless hour in the library pretending to study, but I was really just checking my phone and writing inane notes in my notebook.

At six, I spotted Losia deep in conversation with the head librarian, and I remembered my promise to investigate Carnelian. I decided to see if the nurse had gone home for the day.

Tracing my path back to the healing wing, I found my parents standing in Professor Carnelian's room, silent. They looked as though they'd been that way for hours, still as stone without being in their stone forms.

As I stepped into the room, their eyes shifted to focus on me. Otherwise, they remained motionless. No hugs and not even a handshake.

"What brings you?" Mother asked, voice emotionless.

Her eyes swept me up and down, and I felt a moment of panic.

Could she smell the sex on me? No, we'd showered.

Maybe I looked different? Meri always talked about some weird phenomenon called the afterglow. But didn't you have to go all the way to glow?

The slight tightening of the skin around her eyes told me I was taking too long to answer.

Don't be suspicious, don't be suspicious... I repeated it like a mantra in my mind.

"I wish to inquire as to the health of Professor Carnelian. Has there been any change?" I kept my voice flat, as though I were bored.

If they knew the way my heart was breaking at the sight of my mentor's body withering away, I would be whisked away, and they would probably never update me about his fate.

"Yes," Mother said, and my hope soared. "He's grown worse."

My hope crashed to the ground like a bird flying into a plate-glass window.

"I see." With effort, I kept my tears at bay and ignored the burn behind my eyes.

There was silence for a few moments, and then Father spoke. "Anything else?"

"No. Thank you." I turned and headed back down the

hall, ignoring a dirty look from the nurse who'd chased me out a few hours ago.

When I was back on the lawn, I texted Thane. *Meet at Lycan Hall for dinner?*

The sky was still a sunny, bright blue, but the shadows were growing long, and it was getting cold.

My phone buzzed. *Ok.*

"Short and sweet, I guess," I muttered and set off toward Lycan Hall.

Thane was there waiting for me when I arrived, for which I was grateful. I still didn't understand how the seating arrangements worked.

People just sat themselves down anywhere there was a spare seat, joining whatever argument, joke, or rowdy song was going on. No one seemed to think it was weird to have people inserting themselves into a conversation.

In gargoyle etiquette, such behavior would be considered ill-mannered and boorish. Of course, gargoyles didn't sing or tell jokes either.

I made my way to Thane's dim corner and sat down across from him. He was wearing a navy sweater with a collared shirt beneath. It made him look oddly preppy and reminded me of the first time I'd seen him.

"Do you ever sit with the others?" I realized I'd never really seen Thane be sociable. Who were his friends?

"Sometimes," he answered. "News about Carnelian?"

He wouldn't look at me, let alone smile at me. His finger tapped on the table.

"What's wrong?" I asked.

Thane shrugged. "Nothing," he said, but his mouth twisted in a bitter line.

"Did Kaya make you mad this morning? I'm so sorry, I'll tell her off—"

"No one made me mad." Thane folded his arms over his chest and leaned back.

"And yet, you're clearly mad." I was struggling not to become frustrated. Emotion wouldn't serve me well here.

"Know me so well, do you?" he snapped.

I thought about it, chewing on the inside of my cheek.

"I do know you, and I want to know you better," I answered honestly.

Surprise flashed in his eyes but was quickly replaced by a scowl. "Are you so sure about that, Miss Gargoyle with Feelings?"

I drew back as though he'd bitten me.

"Sorry. I shouldn't have said that." His fists clenched. "I'm not hungry."

He stood abruptly and headed toward the door.

Well, whatever bee was stinging his butt, I wasn't going to let him storm off without explaining it.

I followed him out of Lycan Hall and toward the woods. "Whatever the matter is, we cannot resolve it without communicating. Are you angry with me?"

"I'm not angry!" he growled.

I stopped and crossed my arms. "You are being a stubborn man, but I am a gargoyle, and I guarantee you cannot win a standoff with me. I can turn to stone right here, right now, and wait you out."

"Fine." Thane ran a hand through his hair, perhaps realizing how ridiculous he sounded.

He was breathing hard and kicked at a tree stump with the ball of his Oxford-clad foot. "I'm angry. I'm angry with myself. Are you happy? Of course you're not happy because you're not supposed to feel anything. But from now on, I can promise you, nothing but business between us."

"But I don't understand." I hated how small my voice sounded.

A sudden memory popped into my mind of Meg's one and only fling after her long-term boyfriend left her. She'd gushed the morning after they'd had sex for the first time. Then he'd never spoken to her again.

Was that how Thane felt about me? Had I been a conquest? A point of pride? Did he just want to brag that he got the rigid gargoyle chick in bed?

"Because it's wrong, all right?" He paced between the trees, still refusing to look at me. "It was wrong from the start. You laid out the rules, the scheme, the fake dating, everything. And you offered to help me with my powers, and I took it too far. I took advantage of you when you were emotionally vulnerable. All because I was too horny and stupid to think logically. I'm scum, and I swear I won't do it again."

CHAPTER 16

VELA

"I ... what?" I stared at him. "Thane..."

I stepped toward him, but he only glared and kept pacing again.

"You didn't take advantage of me, Thane. I..." My words tangled in my throat, and my blush spread to the tips of my ears. "I wanted everything that happened last night. Everything I did, and everything you did."

Thane was shaking his head, his eyes alight with anguish. "But you can't know that! My powers give me the ability to heighten emotion. Manipulating what others feel. What if I did that to you?"

I saw the flash of truth in his eyes.

Thane hated himself. He'd spent so long hating himself that he couldn't even stop when his powers finally manifested the way he'd so desperately wanted.

He just found a new way to hate himself.

I'd never talked someone down from a proverbial ledge before. Gargoyles weren't really known for our therapeutic conversational skills or our pep talks. Carnelian was probably the closest to a gargoyle therapist that had ever existed. But no one else could do this but me.

I stepped forward again, grass crunching beneath my converse. Catching one of his wrists, I pulled it away from his hair. Then, did the same with the other.

Lacing my fingers between his, I looked up at him, meeting his eye, and held it.

"I feel," I told him as gently as I could. "I'm pretty sure all gargoyles do, and they just deny it. And I alone choose how I feel. You can make my feelings stronger, but you can't create them out of nothing. If I was afraid of you or disgusted by what was happening between us, don't you think you would've enhanced those feelings, too?"

"I don't know," Thane whispered, raw anguish in his voice.

His fingers tightened around mine, holding me tightly as though he was afraid I'd run.

"Well, I'm sure you can smell me, and scents don't lie. How do I smell right now?"

Thane closed his eyes briefly. "Confused. Piney. Like you."

"If you think I only want you because you planted the emotion, then try to drain me. Right now," I challenged him.

A line appeared between his brow, and he took a deep

breath. A moment later, I felt the dimming of that warm spark in my chest that I was beginning to suspect was love.

As it waned, I focused on Thane and everything I loved about him. His smile, when he wasn't being sarcastic. The warmth of his arms around me. His support as he helped me think logically and do what was right.

My emotions were sucked away, feeding him, but as soon as they began to fade, I'd look into his eyes and remember the way he'd held Sapphire or the gentleness of his paintbrushes on my skin, and the emotions kept coming.

The warmth in my chest grew stronger and brighter until it was too much for him to keep up with. My heart belonged to him, and I knew he was mine.

Thane gasped, and a smokey fog swirled around him in the half-light of dusk. Sharp claws emerged from the end of his fingers, then just as quickly turned back to smooth skin. Fur rippled up his neck and face, then receded.

When he opened his eyes, they were a deep red, like the color of blood. I'd never seen them turn that color before and didn't know what it meant.

"What's happening?" he rasped, his vocal cords raw.

I didn't know, but telling him that wasn't likely to calm him. "You tried to stop me from caring about you. But you couldn't, because my feelings are real. Everything about the way I feel for you is real."

I leaned up, capturing his mouth with mine. This time, I took the lead, parting his lips with my tongue and deepening our kiss.

His mouth was sweet and warm. Shivers raced down my spine, and my body sent wet heat rushing between my thighs as I remembered how it felt to have his mouth licking and tasting me.

I wasn't the only one affected by our kiss, if the hard length pressed against my belly was any sign. We broke apart, panting hard.

"I want you," I confessed quietly.

"Really?" His teeth flashed white as he smiled.

"I think you know the answer to that."

His cock twitched in response. Still, I knew he needed me to say it again.

"Will you come home with me?" I flushed, remembering Meri's teasing. "Though maybe this time I'll scream into a pillow?"

We practically ran to the house, and the door to my room was barely shut before I was pulling off my coat and shirt and leaving them in an untidy heap. Gargoyles never left their rooms messy, and it thrilled me to think I had something more important on my mind.

I pulled Thane's shirt off, then his pants. He divested me of my bra and panties. We stood for a few moments, naked, simply staring at each other.

His frame was long and slender, like the body of a swimmer or marathon runner. I could see the shape of his ribs, the long muscles of his thighs.

He stroked the side of my breast, and a golden spark of longing lit his eyes. Tugging him by the hand, I pulled him over to the bed.

Thane started at my ankle and kissed his way up to the top of my thigh. His tongue found my clitoris, and one of his long fingers stroked up and down my entrance in time with his tongue.

My head lolled back on the pillow, and I allowed the sensation to carry me to some new place. His finger slipped inside of me, and I gasped, my walls clenching and squeezing it.

He worked me gently, bringing me to the edge of bliss over and over until, at last, he sent me over the edge with an earth-shattering orgasm. When he rose over my body to kiss me, I caught sight of his cock, thick and glistening with his own desire. It was a sight so beautiful I had to bite my lip.

"I want you inside me," I whispered against his mouth.

He froze, and I could feel uncertainty warring within him.

"Please, Thane. I know what I want," I assured him.

"Do you know how sexy you are when you say please like that?" he groaned into my neck.

"Please," I begged, arching against him.

Thane drew back. His eyes were serious, and his hand gentle as it stroked my cheek. "You've never done this before, have you?"

"No. Sex wasn't something I had given much thought to until you came into my life." My face flushed. "Does that bother you?"

His smile was dark and feral. "I don't want you to be anyone's but mine," he growled.

The raw lust in his voice called to something primal inside me. I wanted to wrap my legs around his back and pull him in as deep as he could go.

He swallowed hard. "It's probably going to hurt, Vela. I just want you to be sure. And we should go slow at first, so you can get used to me."

I nodded.

Thane drew back, leaving me suddenly cold, and guided my legs apart. He let his cock slide along the length of my opening, drawing a moan from my throat.

"Breathe," he coaxed.

On my exhale, he pressed into me.

He was right. It really freaking hurt.

Thane stilled his forward motion, giving me time to adjust as his mouth distracted me by teasing my aching breasts.

"Okay, you can keep going," I whispered.

"Keep breathing," Thane reminded me.

As he buried himself deeper, desire and pain mingled within me. But then his mouth found my nipple again, and desire trumped the pain. My wings twitched.

Thane eased out a little. "All right?"

I responded by clenching my muscles around his length and smiling at his gasp. Then he let go of my hand and ran a finger along the edge of my wing. The next time he thrust forward, tingling pleasure swept through me.

Seeing that I was no longer in pain, Thane tucked his cheek against mine and began rocking his hips in a steady rhythm. He was slow and gentle, giving his hands plenty of time to explore the erogenous zones on my wings.

"Vela," he breathed.

"Yes," I whispered, though I wasn't sure whether I was saying *yes* to the feeling or to him. It didn't matter. I would say yes to anything he asked of me.

"From the moment I smelled you, I knew you were mine," he said. A thrill shot all the way to my core. "You smell like everything free and beautiful in the world. You're everything I want."

I wrapped my legs up around his back, pulling him tighter against me. My fingers dug into his shoulders. "Yes. I'm yours."

His thrusts quickened, and his growl held a feral edge. "I can't stop."

"Don't stop," I whispered.

The pain was entirely gone now, and pleasure was building to a crescendo. I began to rock my hips, greedy for more of him. My wings wrapped around us, enfolding his back. I whimpered and moaned at the sensations rippling through me, at every brush of his skin against them.

Thane's face contorted, his pace becoming frantic. He licked his thumb, and the moment he touched my clitoris, my world exploded.

I let my head fall back, aware of nothing but the heat of his body and the intensity of my orgasm. My muscles contracted, milking his cock and causing Thane to bite his lip hard enough to draw blood. With three savage thrusts, he collapsed on top of me, his muscles jerking as he joined me in absolute bliss.

His breath tickled my neck, and I could still feel his cock twitching inside me. My wings acted as a blanket for us, cocooning us in our own world. I could feel his heart pounding against mine.

"Are you okay?" His voice was rough.

"I don't think I've ever been better," I admitted breathlessly. "Though I think it's going to be hard to do *that* three times a night."

Thane lifted his head. "For you, I will. A dog does his best to serve, after all."

He smiled as though it were funny, but something about it saddened me.

"I'm not your master." I ran a hand through his hair.

"But you could tell me to do anything, and I'd do it." His expression turned serious. "Anything, Vela."

Hmmm… *anything?*

His cock twitched again, as though it could read my naughtiest thoughts, and he laughed. "Even that."

"Just… lie with me." I pulled him back down and rolled so that we lay on our sides together.

We were close enough that I could feel the beat of his heart against my chest. Close enough to feel a comfortable intimacy. Close enough that I could drape my wing over us both and pretend that the outside world, with its outside problems and outside expectations, didn't even exist.

CHAPTER 17

VELA

Spring sunlight slanted through my window, persistent in its quest to force me into admitting it was morning. That my glorious night was over.

Thane and I were pressed together in a tangle of blankets and wings. Heat seeped from him, warming my body so I felt flushed even though I was naked and only the sheet was still on the bed.

He looked peaceful in sleep, his long black eyelashes brushing his cheeks. I was once again shocked by his sharp-featured beauty. Unable to resist the urge to touch him, I traced a finger down his arm.

Thane cracked open an eyelid.

"Good morning," I whispered, feeling suddenly shy.

In the dark, it had been easier to voice what I wanted and explore his body.

He had none of those issues. "It is a good morning, because I woke up with you in my arms."

Thane's hand found my hip, and then we were rolling. When we stopped, I found myself on top, straddling his hips. "Ready for a second round?"

From my new position, I was able to run my fingers from his belly button over the slim plane of his stomach, down to the V at his legs... and the cock that stirred beyond.

I leaned forward to kiss him, angling my hips up so that he could work his cock inside me. As he lined himself up against my entrance, my stomach gave an almighty gurgle, demanding sustenance.

"Sorry," I groaned, pressing my face against his chest so he couldn't see my embarrassment.

"For what?" Thane laughed. "Let's get you something to eat. I'm probably on the verge of missing another class, anyway. We'll just have to sneak home for lunch sex like everyone else does."

Sitting up, I gently lifted his shoulders so I could free my wings from where they were partly pinned beneath him. I stretched them as best I could in the small room before tucking them back against my body. Gargoyle wings were impressively large and were equally impressive in their ability to compact incredibly well.

I eyed him suspiciously as I stood and began searching for my clothes. "Everybody? You act as though everyone at Slaymore is perpetually horny."

"We're young adults in college. Everyone here *is* perpetually horny and looking for opportunities to copulate." He slid into his boxers and then his jeans.

When he looked up, I caught the glint of mischief in his eyes and realized he was teasing me.

I scrunched my nose in disgust. "Don't call it that."

"Why? Isn't that what you called it not too long ago?" He pulled me to my feet.

"Because—" I grabbed my bra from the floor, trying to figure out why I hated the way it sounded.

Thane took the bra from my hands and turned me to face away from him. He slid a cup over each breast, then brushed my hair to the side so he could hook it. The care he was showing me was sensual but also tender, and suddenly I knew why I didn't like the word.

"Copulate sounds cold and unfeeling." I turned, wrapping my arms around him and resting my cheek against his chest. "I felt everything, and I don't want to degrade it with such an impersonal word."

Just the softest touch from Thane could turn my stony body into molten lava. I wanted nothing more than to tumble back into bed with him, but at the last moment, I remembered my parents were on campus and grabbed a collared shirt from my wardrobe.

Parents. That single word put a damper on my sex drive.

How long did they intend to stay? And how much were they intending to monitor me while they did?

At least Thane could help me with my emotions, but I'd barely convinced them our relationship was professional before. I shook my head, trying to clear the panic with logic.

There was no way I would be able to hide my happiness after spending a night in Thane's arms. But as long as I got him to feed from me and drain some of those emotions before we left the house this morning, I'd be fine.

I followed him down the stairs.

As we came into the kitchen, he said, "Wow. Cooking for an army?"

"I like to cook," came Kaya's voice. "Also, I tend to stress cook."

"What are you stressed about?" I asked, trying my best to keep the pink from my cheeks.

I had nothing to be ashamed of. Kaya knew Thane and I were together, and it wasn't like she had no sexual experience herself.

The kitchen looked as though a bomb had gone off... a cake bomb. Every mixing bowl in the house dripped with cake batter, egg whites, or frosting. A thin layer of flour dusted almost every surface. The oven was on, but instead of cake, a casserole dish full of pancakes was keeping warm inside.

I heard the telltale thud of Meri's feet on the stairs and turned toward her.

"Mmm. I smell breakfast," she declared, her voice groggy. "Is there coffee?"

She trudged in, her hair a wild tangle around her face. Meri was so intent on reaching the coffee maker that she nearly stepped on Thane's foot. It was only after she'd poured herself a cup and taken a long, satisfied drink that she even noticed we were there.

"You." She pointed with her mug at Thane. "I remember you."

"Uh… good? May I?" Thane gestured to the coffeepot.

"I hope you're treating our girl well." Meri handed it over, and I found a clean mug for Thane to use.

Thane shot me an amused glance. "Is she giving me the Dad talk?"

"What?" Meri furrowed her brow.

Her eyes were red-rimmed, making me wonder when she'd gotten to bed last night.

"You know, the Dad talk. 'Rules for dating my daughter' and all that," Thane joked.

"That sexist crap?" Meri had already finished her first cup of coffee and quickly poured herself a second. She was looking better by the moment as the caffeine hit her system. "Nah. I will tell you, though. If you make her cry…"

"You'll make me cry?" Thane lifted his coffee cup in salute.

"No. Of course not." Meri lifted one foot and wiggled her talons. "I'll rip you apart with my feet. Got it?"

Thane gulped his coffee and choked. "I think this coffee is going to kill me first." His eyes watered. "How does Kaya make it? Three parts coffee, two parts sludge? Did you actually add water, or did you just find a way to melt the beans directly?"

Meri narrowed her eyes and pursed her lips. She glared at him for a long moment, then laughed.

"All right." She clapped him on the back hard enough to

send him stumbling and coffee sloshing over the rim of his cup and onto the floor.

I probably only imagined that the toxic liquid hissed as it made contact with the linoleum.

"I liked you yesterday, and I still like you today. Good sign." Her smile dropped, and her voice turned dark. "Seriously, though. Rip. You. Apart."

Thane slid an arm around my waist and pulled me close. It would have been sweet if I didn't think he might be using me as a shield.

"I really don't think you're going to have that problem," he said. "I will help you rip apart anyone who upsets our girl."

"Sounds like a party!" Meri grinned.

"Does she always wake up and choose violence?" Thane murmured against my ear.

"Always." I giggled and caught the knowing twinkle in Meri's eyes as she sipped her cup of caffeinated bitterness.

Kaya clapped her hands. "Pancakes and coffee. And there's a chocolate cake in the fridge. And I thought I could make blueberry muffins for a snack, and—"

"By all that's holy, Kaya, go take a walk. You've got five hours until you can get your results, and you will not spend them all cooped up in here baking." Meri gently pushed her out of the kitchen. "I'll clean up."

Meri brought the pancakes to the table while I grabbed the plates and cutlery.

"What results is Kaya waiting for?" Thane asked as he found napkins for all of us.

"Her second-to-last Magical Law exam," I explained. "If she gets over 90 percent, her overall average for the class means she automatically qualifies for the internship she got. She'll be officially in."

"She's never gotten less than a 95 in anything, so I don't understand why she's so worked up," Meri grumbled as she opened the fridge and pulled out the cake. "On the other hand, cake for breakfast is a definite perk of living with Kaya."

The stairs creaked as Meg came down.

"Morning." She yawned, pulling her hair back in a loose ponytail and adjusting her glasses. "Don't go out in the rain today."

I looked at the cloud-free sky out the kitchen window.

"Why not?" asked Thane, taking another sip of his coffee and wincing.

"The horoscope didn't tell me why. But it bore a bad omen with rainfall." She sagged down on the seat across from me. "Pass the jam, please."

For a few minutes, we were silent, stuffing Kaya's delicious pancakes into our mouths. I took pity on Thane and got out the cream and sugar. I watched as he poured until the coffee was a lovely light color that made him sigh in pleasure.

When he'd finished his fourth pancake, he leaned back in his chair. "How did you all become roommates, anyway?"

"It's Meri's fault," Meg said placidly and toyed with her necklace.

Meri swallowed a bite of cake. "She's right. It is my fault. I knew all these lovely ladies and each of them was a little cracked and needed something special. Meg needed a place where she didn't have to remember the loser she dumped. Kaya needed a house with a good kitchen and her own room for privacy. Vela needed to be with people who could get her out of her shell. And I had already agreed to rent this place, so I more or less sat the girls down and told them they were living with me."

"Just like that?" Thane sounded impressed.

Meri smiled, and in the morning light, her sharp teeth glinted. "I can be very persuasive."

Before Thane could respond, there was a quick succession of taps at the window. A crow sat on the sill, frantically pecking on the glass.

I pushed my chair back and hurried over, unlatching the window and holding out my arm for the bird to hop on.

The sky that had been a bright baby blue was now dark. How had the sky clouded over so quickly?

I bit my lip, casting a worried glance back at Meg, then lifted the bird to eye height.

My magic swirled between us, and visions flashed before me in a series of successive images. I saw my parents flanking Professor Carnelian's hospital bed. A frown was on Mother's face as she looked down at a leather journal, mouthing something.

Then she looked up and locked eyes with the bird directly. *Come,* she mouthed soundlessly.

I knew that was meant for me. She'd sent the crow to fetch me.

Fear clogged my throat as I stared at her hard, angry face. Mother never showed emotion, so I couldn't imagine what had happened to make a gargoyle like her show anger.

"I have to go." I clenched my jaw and fought to bring my cold, gargoyle exterior to the surface.

Thane stood, concern flashing in his red eyes. "Should I come with you?"

I shook my head. "It's my parents. I'll tell you what I find out."

Having delivered his message, the crow took flight; I shut the window behind him, then hurried over to the front door and slipped my feet into my shoes.

As I pulled on my jacket, Thane appeared before me. His fingers closed lightly around my wrist. My breath caught as his thumb rubbed against my pulse.

He leaned forward, and I felt the swirl of his magic across my skin before his lips claimed mine in a fierce, quick kiss. My desire flared, adding to the emotional hurricane spinning inside me.

Then, they vanished, leaving nothing but quiet calm behind.

"Thank you." I tilted my chin, acknowledging the favor he'd done for me.

Thane ran his thumb across my cheek, then stepped back with a sad smile. "You're welcome."

Without another word, I opened the door and set off across the grounds just as the first fat drops of rain pattered on the trees above me.

CHAPTER
18

VELA

I presented myself to my parents with a curt nod. They were still dressed in yesterday's clothes. Somehow, neither of them had a hair out of place, despite the fact that I knew they hadn't slept last night.

The spike of nerves I would normally feel when dealing with my parents was, thankfully, dull as an old knife. I glanced at the bed, catching sight of Carnelian, and even with my emotions dampened, sorrow throbbed in my chest.

The old gargoyle looked sunken and corpse-like. I stepped forward, wanting to check his extremities for signs of scleroderma. But before I'd taken two steps, my mother raised the leather book I'd seen in my vision.

"Have you read this?"

"No," I replied flatly. "The professor used a different

notebook in our lessons. I have never had cause to go through his things."

Except when Thane and I had snuck into his apartment, but that felt like a lifetime ago.

"These seem to be his private musings. And alarmingly, most are about you," Father got straight to the point, his purple eyes watching my face for... what? Guilt? Sadness?

My mind went blank. "I... don't understand."

Mother flipped to a random page. *"Twenty-ninth September of last year: 'Vela was unhappy today, and it rained.' First of October: 'Vela was in high spirits, and the sun was bright and warm.'"*

She flipped back several pages. *"First April last year: 'Roses are unseasonably in bloom. Weather has been warmer than usual. Vela pretends to be more advanced than she is in our proposed studies. Therefore, she is not always forthcoming with her moods, but evidence suggests that a connection exists between the local weather patterns and the emotional state of the gargoyle female. I suspect it is a type of empathetic connection.'* Do you have any idea what he means?"

The way she asked it put me on high alert. It was as though the question were a test, and I was supposed to know the answer.

I replayed what she'd read in my mind, turning the words carefully over in my mind. "Is Professor Carnelian suggesting I can control Slaymore's weather?"

The muscles in my father's jaw jerked. It was a sign of agitation or anger I'd often observed in mundanes and the other students, but I'd never seen it in a gargoyle.

"What was he teaching you, girl?" Father snapped. "Stop wasting valuable time and tell the truth."

I took a controlling breath and steeled my voice to prevent a wobble. "I visited Professor Carnelian three times a week to train emotion suppression and logical thought."

"Would you swear that before the council?" Mother snapped.

"Of course." I clasped my hands in front of me to ensure they wouldn't start trembling.

Even with my drained emotions, my parents' loss of control was terrifying. And why did they want me to swear in front of the council? That was a serious thing.

It seemed as though they were accusing me of committing some type of crime. "What is happening?"

Mother flipped through the journal some more. "Listen carefully." She cleared her throat and read. "'Before the existence of the Gargoyle Council, no one chose a gargoyle for a city. Gargoyles were said to choose the cities themselves, but that wasn't completely accurate. It was the cities that made the choice.

"'Gargoyles who loved a city and formed a special bond could be selected by that city as its protector or guardian. In such cases, their skill with emotions aided them in feeling a city's needs and wants and fulfilling them accurately. It is what I believe happened to me decades ago with Slaymore. And as our newest gargoyle student continues to flourish here, I worry the same will happen to her.

"If the city forms a bond with her, the consequences would be immeasurable for my body. Yet this was the natural way of our species. In days passed, the life cycle of a gargoyle often ended *with the advent of a new protector chosen by the city. Perhaps a young town like Slaymore requires a young gargoyle to meet its needs fully. I have lived a long life—a life which I hesitantly say I have enjoyed.'"*

I bit down on my tongue, desperately trying to keep my tears at bay as she continued to read.

"'I must carefully consider whether I wish to disrupt the natural order of things and change the course of a young life. A choice which could be potentially catastrophic.'"

Mother looked up at me, her dark eyes inscrutable. "Do you understand what Professor Carnelian is saying in these pages?"

I felt light, as though my body might begin floating toward the ceiling at any moment. My head spun, and I longed to sit down, but there were no chairs in the room.

"Am I..." Despite my best efforts to remain stoic, my body swayed. "Have I been chosen? No, that's impossible. Slaymore's not a city, and it doesn't need a guardian. It already has one."

But if what Carnelian suspected was true, it meant I'd passed the greatest test a gargoyle could have. I'd been deemed worthy by a magic far greater than that of the Gargoyle Council.

Mother flipped forward again in the journal until she found the most recent entry. *"'Tonight, I felt the beat of the city weaken. It has been my constant companion for many decades, but it has become clear that its allegiance is shifting to Vela. It won't be long now before the bond between them is completed.*

"'Despite my efforts, I've found little information on how the

heart of a city works. One thing that every document on the topic agrees on is that the old guardian must die for the new guardian to assume their place and protect the city properly. I already feel more tired in my bones, less strong. Without the heartbeat to sustain me, my body cannot continue.'"

I struggled to remain upright as the air was sucked from my lungs.

It was my fault, and because of me, Carnelian lay dying.

Mother continued, but her voice sounded as though I were hearing it from underwater. *"'I will tell Vela tomorrow, and together, we will discuss how to approach the council. She can, perhaps, help me gather my notes and put together a more coherent paper on the methods of natural guardian selection. Vela's open love of Slaymore has strengthened her, and in turn, her bond with the city has grown stronger.*

"'Perhaps, in the wake of this case study, it is time that our species rethinks the importance we have placed on living a cold and emotionless life. And more importantly, we need to reevaluate the ethical implications of forcing that lifestyle onto the next generation of guardians.'"

Mother's voice had gone hoarse, and Father handed her a glass of water. Both of them glared at me, waiting for my response.

I stood frozen, unable to breathe because of the emotions tearing at my insides like a school of ravenous piranhas.

My mind flashed back to the pulse I'd felt in the midst of Slaymore. I'd used my magic to soothe its erratic beat.

That had been the heart of the city, calling to me. And I'd answered.

A tear slid down my cheek, but I didn't bother trying to wipe it away. "When did he write that?" I whispered, my voice cracking.

"Three days ago. Do you still claim that he never told you?" Mother's nostrils flared.

"He collapsed that night." He must have been planning to tell me when I'd returned from my watch.

But I'd stopped those boys from their ill-timed break-in, and the city had made her decision...

My tear-filled eyes ran over the thin, wan form in the bed.

I was killing Professor Carnelian.

"Whether or not you knew is something for the council to judge," Father decided. "Our assignment was to assess whether Professor Carnelian's death could be prevented, and it can. We will withdraw you from Slaymore at once. If his theories are correct, the city will revert to her old guardian when you go."

Mother closed the notebook with finality. "At least we know these last four years haven't been a waste, even if you still struggle to keep your disgraceful displays to yourself." She gestured at my face. "It is unheard of for a city to reach out to form a bond with a guardian. That is an impressive feat for one your age. The council may even see fit to assign you to another city immediately."

Immediately. I was leaving Slaymore.

She thought I could just bond with another city because the council decreed it, which showed she didn't understand how that type of bond was created.

"I… How long do I have?" I asked in a shaky voice.

"We'll leave as soon as you've settled your affairs. It should hardly take long." Mother glanced at the tiny gold watch on her wrist. "Let's meet at the front gate in fifteen minutes."

Fifteen minutes.

In fifteen minutes, the life I'd built would be nothing but a painful memory.

Spinning on my heels, I ran.

CHAPTER 19

VELA

A s I ran out of the healing wing, rain poured down in full force, plastering my hair to my skull and my clothes to my body.

I stumbled, nearly tumbling to the muddy graveled path, and decided I didn't have time to walk. Not with my entire life falling apart. Jerking my wings open, I took to the sky.

As I soared over the treetops, my tears mixed with the raindrops that were pelting my skin like a thousand stinging bees. But that discomfort was nothing compared to the heart-wrenching pain that had left my heart in tatters.

I was a disgraced gargoyle who was more likely to receive a collar upon graduation than a position anywhere in gargoyle society, yet the heart of a city had picked me. It had wanted me.

But that meant Carnelian, the only gargoyle who hadn't treated me as defective and who had—in his own way— showed me more care than my parents, lay dying. All because of me.

I had to leave to save him, but I knew without a doubt that leaving here was going to break me in ways that could never be repaired.

Last night, I'd been so happy. I'd even dared to let myself dream of a future with Thane. Now, I realized the absolute foolishness of those thoughts. He was like a Renaissance statue, made of intricately carved marble and protected inside museums for people to admire. My species had been portrayed well by gothic architecture. We were placed on top of cathedrals, meant to weather hardship and storms, our grotesque open-mouthed grimaces scaring away evil. We were protectors who were meant to spend our lives alone. Watching but never experiencing.

Carnelian had been wrong. Emotions were a terrible thing. Without them, gargoyles wouldn't realize how lonely they were or how gray their existence on Earth truly was.

The moment the house came into view, I folded my wings, dropping into a steep dive. I half-tumbled through the trees and landed in a heap on the soaked grass beside the porch.

Gathering myself, I tried to push to my feet but couldn't find the strength. I curled up on my side and covered myself with my wing to hide my shame as I sobbed.

Barely a minute had passed before the front door

groaned, and Thane dropped to the ground beside me, not even caring about the mud and water soaking his pants.

"Vela! Are you hurt?" His hand gently folded back my wing, tucking it against my back as his eyes flicked over my face, assessing.

He quickly understood that my cheeks weren't just wet from the rain and lifted me into his arms as he carried me inside. "Love, what's going on?"

Unable to speak, I fisted my hand in his shirt and clung to him, sobbing. Thane's arms tightened, holding me tight as water from my tears and drenched clothing soaked through his sleeves.

"It's all right, Vela," he murmured, pressing his lips to my soaked hair. "Whatever's going on, you can tell me." He pulled back, and his eyes flared, reminding me of how a campfire reacted when a fresh log was tossed in it. "Is it your parents?" Thane's voice dropped, and he whispered, "Let's not tell Meri because I want to kill them myself. If she finds out they made you cry, she'll try to get to them first. She's really itching to use her feet."

At his unexpected joke, my sob turned into a laugh. But that only lasted for a moment before sadness snuffed out that tiny flicker of amusement, leaving me to drown in sorrow again.

How could I tell Thane I was the reason his father figure was dying?

He would hate me. I was going to leave campus knowing the first person I'd ever loved now despised me.

Yet I couldn't lie to him. He deserved the truth.

"Come on." He peeled my coat off, then my shirt.

"What're you doing?" I hiccupped, tugging at the hem and glancing around the kitchen to see if my roommates were nearby.

Thane took off my wet shoes and socks, then draped his coat around me. "We've all seen you naked. I'll be right back. Wait here."

Kicking off his shoes, he disappeared up the stairs.

I heard him knock on a door, then the murmur of voices. A few moments later, he was coming down the stairs again, equipped with Meri's fluffiest, pinkest robe.

"She said it was warm." He pulled off the coat and settled the robe on my shoulders.

The fabric was soft, lined with some kind of feather that tickled the back of my neck. It was at least a foot too long, but when Thane led me to the kitchen and set me on a chair, it was perfect for wrapping around my freezing body.

I watched as he moved confidently around the kitchen. When had he become so comfortable here? He'd only had a couple of days to get used to it. Yet he moved with precision, somehow finding my favorite cup, a saucepan, and a packet of hot chocolate.

"I have to tell you something," I began, but he held up a finger.

"First, the chocolate. It was the number one healer of ailments in Hades for mistreated boys who were hiding from their parents, and I got to be a pro at making it. Once you've had a little drink, then we can talk."

"But my parents will be here in…" I checked the clock. "Ten minutes."

"Then I'll sic Meri on them until we've had a chance to sort this out. It will be all right, my love."

He'd called me his love.

And the words had rolled off his tongue so easily, so confidently. It felt natural and right, but I was being forced to leave it behind.

My tears started flowing again, but I managed to cry silently, swiping at my eyes at intervals. Thane set down my hot chocolate and sat down in the chair next to me, scooting it so that he faced me and could rest his palm on my thigh.

I didn't think I could swallow, let alone keep anything down, but when I opened my mouth to protest, he gave me a stern look.

"Drink."

Not having the energy to argue, I drank.

The hot chocolate was good, although I still considered it a frivolous beverage. But since it might be my last chance at frivolity, I decided to enjoy it. It was going to be my last chance at a lot of things.

"You look scared." Thane took my hand, rubbing it between his warm palms. "You don't ever need to be afraid of telling me something, Vela."

That's where you're wrong. I didn't fear his anger. I just didn't think I could survive watching the love in his eyes shift to hatred. But I might as well rip off the Band-Aid, to use Meri's favorite expression.

"It's my fault Professor Carnelian is dying."

Thane cocked his head. "How do you figure that?"

"There's a… myth among gargoyles. That cities come alive, and the gargoyle that can feel a city's heartbeat becomes that city's protector. Chosen by the city to guard it, take care of it, help it grow, and watch it flourish."

I took a deep breath. "For a long time, I have been taught that such a story is nonsense, but I've felt Slaymore's beating heart. It chose me to be its guardian."

"That's incredible, Vela! You're incredible." Thane's hand squeezed mine. "This sounds like a good thing, so why are you crying?"

"Because Professor Carnelian was Slaymore's guardian first," I whispered miserably. "And when the city's magic began reaching for me, he got cut off from it. That's why he started to die."

Grabbing a napkin from the table, I pressed it against my eyes, trying to stop the flow of tears. "My mother read some of his journal entries to me. He'd written that, apparently, it was my emotions that triggered the connection to begin forming. Slaymore sensed how much I loved it here…" I hiccuped. "If we want Professor Carnelian to survive, I have to leave. Immediately."

Thane reached out to pull one of my hands from my eyes. "No. There has to be another way."

"There isn't." In a sudden wave of exasperation, I seized his face with both hands. "Kiss me," I begged. "Take all this mess away. I don't want to feel anymore."

Thane had been leaning forward, ready to grant my request for a kiss, but he reeled back as I finished speaking.

I finally saw the flash of anger in his eyes. "I will not do that."

"Thane." I scooted forward, trying to capture his mouth with mine. He jerked back. "Please, I can't leave like this. Help me take my punishment and reassignment with my chin up and without humiliating myself further."

He stood abruptly, knocking over his chair. "And I don't want you to be punished and reassigned at all. Why would they punish you, anyway?"

"Gargoyle murder is as serious a crime as any other type of murder," I said. "Please, Thane. I can take my punishment, but I can't bear the pain I will feel at losing you and being taken away from Slaymore."

"Hades!" He ran a hand through his dark curls and glared at the ceiling. "Vela, you didn't *murder* him. Things happened. Unfortunate things, but things you didn't understand. You didn't ask the city to pick a new guardian. Surely removing you from Slaymore is only going to make things more unstable here. Don't cities need gargoyles?"

I sniffled into my hot chocolate. "The current hypothesis is that Professor Carnelian will recover if the city turns back to him. And the city will turn back to him if I'm gone. As long as another overly emotional, defective gargoyle doesn't show up and fall in love with Slaymore, he will live."

Taking a steadying breath, I pushed down on all my grief and anger. "If you don't want to help me, I understand. You'll soon have your mentor back, and I ask that you please forgive me for the turmoil I caused in your life."

Thane stood frozen, his jaw slack.

I'd had many years to practice masking my true feelings and presenting myself as a proper gargoyle. It was unimaginably difficult, but I could do it.

Standing, I tried to gather up the fluffy robe. "Thank you for the drink, but I must attend to things. I will be summoned soon, and I have a few others to say goodbye to."

I tried to focus my mind on practical things as I headed toward the stairs. The few clothes I would pack, discussing the rent I'd miss with Meri, making arrangements for Sapphire's care—

"No," Thane said in a low, dangerous voice that sent thrilling shivers all over my body. He stepped in front of me, blocking me from the stairs. "You're not going to do that. Not now."

"Do what?" I asked flatly, ignoring the burn behind my eyes as I fought fresh tears.

"Pretending you have no emotions. You *feel*, Vela. I've seen how full of joy, passion, and life you are. And you have the right to feel all those things."

"No, I don't." Despite my best efforts, my voice wobbled. "You can see what happens when a gargoyle feels. Slaymore town is in turmoil, people have lost their livelihoods, and someone we both care for is on his deathbed. This is, perhaps, the most salient lesson in emotions I have ever had." I snorted a quiet laugh and swallowed the sob that tried to follow it. "And I've learned it."

Thane's hand slipped from the doorframe to my shoulder, then down my arm. He tenderly intertwined his fingers with mine.

"Your emotions led you to completion," he said quietly. "Slaymore chose you because of your emotion and your caring heart. I understand it can feel easier to live without emotion. Believe me, I *understand.*" He lifted my hand and kissed the back of it. "But living without them means living without a beautiful part of yourself. And you know that now."

I shook my head. "It's possible I'll still be assigned a city to protect. I can still do what I was meant to do without involving my heart."

As long as the council didn't declare me a threat to the very foundation of modern gargoyle society and turn me to stone for a hundred years. At the thought of the stone sentence, all the feelings I'd been trying to suppress surged up with a vengeance.

I'd be trapped for a hundred years, my body stone, but my mind reliving every memory I'd made at Slaymore... over and over. I'd be watching the world pass me by as Thane, Meri, Meg, and Kaya moved on with their lives and left me alone.

"All the other gargoyles can do it with ease." Angry tears slipped from my eyes as my voice rose. "Why can't I? Why can't I be a *proper* gargoyle?"

Thane leaned forward and kissed me gently on the forehead. His eyes had dimmed to a burnished, soft copper. He drew me into his embrace, his hand cradling my head against his chest.

"You can't be all other gargoyles. You can only be you." He held me steady there, solid as a stone, ready to hold me up for as long as I needed. "And you are a proper gargoyle," he told me softly. "You're so proper you didn't need an idiotic committee to tell you that you're worthy of being a guardian. You're such an incredible gargoyle that the very earth recognized you and wanted to bond. And apparently, that is so rare it's believed to be a myth. That makes you a legend."

I gave a watery laugh. "Well, Professor Carnelian is one, too. That's how we got into all this trouble in the first place. I guess he believed it was a magic that had been lost or that he'd been mistaken about the city being alive. Gargoyles get reassigned all the time without dying, but that's because their magic isn't entwined with the heart of their city."

He drew back so we could see eye to eye again. "Listen. We can go to Losia. Now that we know what's wrong with Carnelian, we can talk to her about a cure. This is one of the best places for paranormals to be sick. I'm sure she'll dig down to look for a cure."

Three sharp, precise raps sounded at the door, causing us to jump. I glanced at the clock, even though I knew what it would say. My time was up, and I should have met my parents five minutes ago.

"I'll get it," came Meri's voice.

"I should get it—" I tried to scoot past Thane, but he gently shook his head and held me in place with a hand on my arm.

I crossed my arms, only to have something soft and fluffy tickle my skin.

Fulgurite!

My parents were going to see me in the most ridiculous, un-gargoyle-like robe in existence. This could only go poorly.

The door creaked open. "Can I help you with something?" asked Meri in an icy tone that clearly said, *no, I can't*. "Are you...door-to-door salesmen? Unless you're selling dragon-sized dildos, I'm not interested."

"I'm Corata, and we were told this was Vela Kyanite's place of residence," came Mother's flat voice.

"Oh, yeah. Sorry, she's not available right now."

Father raised his voice to call past Meri. "Vela? You're late, and a feathered she-creature blocks our entrance into your residence. Stop wasting valuable time."

"You don't have to go," Thane whispered.

Of course I did. I gave him a sad smile.

"Oh, you're Vela's *parents*. You know, 'feathered she-creature' is one of my better nicknames. But I'm going to have to take offense, anyway," Meri admitted with a dark chuckle. "Because I've been looking for a chance to sharpen my claws on you for, what, a couple of years?"

"I do hope you're not threatening a guest of Slaymore," came an older and much more severe voice.

My eyes widened, and I shot Thane a panicked look. "That's Headmistress Losia. What is she doing here?"

"Uh, hi?" Meri sounded as confused as I felt.

"Hello, Meri," Losia said calmly. "Is Vela in?" Her tone brooked no argument.

"I'm here," I said, ducking under Thane's arm and coming to the door.

I felt, rather than heard, Thane move behind me. His warm, comforting presence gave me the courage to straighten my spine and face my parents and the head-mistress, even while wearing the fluffy pink monstrosity.

Mother's mouth fell open. In the world of gargoyles, that was practically a faint. It would have been humorous if my life wasn't crashing down around me.

"What *are* you wearing?" Father demanded.

Losia noticed Thane behind me. "Oh, good. I don't have to seek both of you out separately. You're needed in the examination hall immediately."

"That won't be necessary, Headmistress," Mother said in her most intimidating voice. "Vela's enrollment in Slaymore is withdrawn as of this moment."

Losia was completely unruffled. "That's nice. She's still required to come to the examination hall. I suspect you'll be wanted there as well. Come."

"Could I change first?" I asked.

"No, we are needed there immediately. Let's go." Losia turned and ushered my parents down the path, clearly expecting us to follow on her heels.

CHAPTER 20

VELA

I t turned out the meeting was being held in the exam hall because it was the only place that could hold us all. I entered behind Mother, Father, and Losia, then froze in shock.

The hall itself was a converted theater, and its stadium seating was equipped with folding desks.

A large stage was at the far end of the room, and the entire Gargoyle Council of almost forty minutes milled about. Their wings rustled, and they looked uncomfortable in human clothing as they conferred in low voices.

The other half of the stage was packed with people I didn't recognize at all. An unusually tall man and the elegant woman who stood at his side caught my attention. Both were dressed in heavily embroidered black robes and looked as pale as the moon.

The couple was surrounded by a small retinue of black-robed people who also looked like they'd gotten lost on the way to a cultist's birthday party... or possibly a blood sacrifice.

Studying the rest of the black-robed figures, a shock of realization flashed through me when my eyes landed on a tall, slim man. The familiar sharp nose and thin mouth gave him away, though his curly-black hair had been smoothed back. His whole face was twisted up with disdain, and an air of violence radiated from him.

"Is that..."

"My family," Thane muttered, answering my unfinished question. "What are *they* doing here?"

Next to the disdainful man stood a pale woman with silky blonde hair and a face like the jagged edge of a mirror. She wore an expression that made it seem like something had died and was rotting under her nose.

Just behind them stood a young man who had to be Thane's exemplary brother. Unlike Thane, this guy resembled his mother more than his father, with sharp features and her pale hair. He didn't seem disdainful; he looked bored.

Thane gently prodded me forward. We approached the stage slowly, and I ran my fingers along the red velvet of the seats as we headed toward the stage.

As we passed the front row of seats, Thane moved out from behind me and lightly hopped up the stage steps. With breathtaking grace, he dropped to one knee.

"My lord," he murmured to the tall, elegant man who must be the Lord of Hades.

"My servant," the man responded.

A young woman who appeared to be around our age stepped forward. She was beautiful, in a pale, deathly sort of way, and she appeared so delicate that I worried she would break if she sneezed.

"Hello, Thane," she said in a voice that chimed like tolling bells.

"Princess."

"Did you have anything to do with this?" She put her hands on her hips. Her scowl was ruined by the twitching at the corner of her mouth and her glittering eyes.

Thane's deep, throaty laugh sent a sudden pang of jealousy stabbing through my heart. This was not the time, so I pushed it down and summoned my gargoyle calm.

It was obvious she was the princess he was set to protect once he left Slaymore. She wasn't some long-lost love or pre-determined match for him. It was natural they would have developed a familiarity, and I was glad to see someone in his life didn't treat him with disdain.

"Did you really bring the entire retinue up to investigate my mentor's illness?" Thane asked.

"Losia alerted me to what was happening here, as death is somewhat my specialty," the Lord of Hades replied for his daughter. "It is nearly unheard of for a gargoyle to die, so I wished to see him myself."

He frowned over at the other side of the room. "I will

admit, I did not expect to find this amount of chaos or for you to be involved."

"There is a reason you have had no gargoyle entrants to the Underworld," a gargoyle stated stiffly, making his way across the stage.

I recognized him as the head of the council, a gargoyle named Baryte. "We do not belong to you. Our deaths are of a different nature."

"Which is the cause for my curiosity." The Lord of Hades lifted one shoulder in a cultured shrug. "A species that doesn't leave Earth upon death to travel to the afterlife realms is intriguing, and very few things intrigue me at my age."

Baryte lifted his chin and opened his mouth, but Losia cleared her throat. Was it just me, or had she grown taller somehow? "If you don't mind, we need to get moving on this. While we are happy to have such illustrious guests visit Slaymore, in the future, an advance notice would be appreciated. I have matters needing my attention and a campus to run."

"We do apologize for the inconvenience," Baryte said in his gravelly voice. "And we thank you for the hospitality. Vela Kyanite, let us speak so we do not waste anymore of the headmistress's valuable time."

With all eyes on me, it was hard to walk up onto the stage. The fact I was wearing what looked like the feathers of a dozen flamingoes made it far, far worse.

It was possible being naked would've been less embarrassing.

I bowed slightly to the Lord of Hades and his contingent. Thane's glowing red eyes locked with mine, and he gave me a brief, reassuring smile.

Finding my calm and doing my best to freeze my emotions as Carnelian had taught me, I turned to face the council.

"Vela… Kyanite," Baryte boomed. "You were enrolled at Slaymore three and a half years ago with the purpose of receiving your higher education while studying gargoyle nature with Professor Carnelian."

"Yes," I replied, feeling the judging eyes of forty gargoyles bearing down on me.

I didn't need psychic abilities to know they didn't appreciate the feathered frivolity I was wearing.

"And what is your opinion of your *progress*?" The slight emphasis in his voice when he said progress made it clear what he thought about it.

I lifted my chin. "Professor Carnelian taught me to dissect my unfortunate human feelings to find their root cause. With diligent practice, I've learned to use meditation and breathing exercises to modulate my emotions and recall the gargoyle way. I am capable of making logical decisions in a quick and efficient manner, both in my daily life and in the special situations for which my gargoyle abilities are needed."

"Indeed?" another council member said.

She had mottled gray and white skin and was the tallest female gargoyle on the stage. One perfect eyebrow arched as she took in my attire.

One look at the faces of the council told me I would never be seen as anything other than a fault within our community. Gargoyles lived a long time, and they were never going to forget my perceived weakness.

Clenching my teeth together, I searched my soul for my gargoyle calm. I found it, but I also found my spine.

"For example, I had removed my wet clothing after becoming drenched in the rain this morning. However, I was summoned here before I could find a more suitable garment. Wasting the time of the important guests gathered here by taking the time to change was illogical."

I kept my face expressionless, but I could practically hear Meri's voice cheering me on in my head. "Embarrassment at one's attire is a rather un-gargoyle-like trait and one I would have suffered from before I began my lessons with Professor Carnelian."

That cleared up a few of the disdainful looks from among the council, I noticed. However, the councilwoman who'd asked seemed unconvinced, as did my parents.

Baryte cleared his throat. "How do you practice the gargoyle lifestyle on a normal day?"

I told them of my sojourns down to Slaymore to sit on the roofs throughout the town and watch over the city. Baryte listened, nodding sagely.

When I told them about my encounter with the would-be thieves and the break-in at *Books and Brews*, someone whispered in Baryte's ear. He held up a finger for me to pause, then turned to confer with several others.

After several minutes of hushed back-and-forth whispers, he turned around again. "And do you feel anything connected to the city?"

I hesitated. How much trouble would I be in if I confessed? Then again, I wanted to save Carnelian, right?

"I… felt something deep within the ground. A pulse. It happened first on the night I stopped the break-in. Then again, when the town suffered a quake."

From somewhere behind me, Losia gasped a soft, "Oh!"

My fingers clenched into fists inside the oversized hot pink sleeves, and I drew a shaky breath. I felt Thane move to stand behind me.

My fingers tingled with gargoyle magic, and I longed to reach back to touch him. Not to have him drain my emotions but to give me strength just with his reassuring presence. I could almost feel the steady beat of his heart, and I wondered if the sound would remain etched into my memory forever.

The council's expressions had turned stone-cold serious. No more sneers at my dress and even the disdainful councilwoman appeared more thoughtful than judgmental.

"And how do you feel *about* the city?" Baryte's pale blue eyes fixed on me with an intense stare.

I hesitated, trying to figure out how to answer honestly while downplaying my emotions.

"We know you struggle with unnecessary emotions, Vela Kyanite," the councilwoman snapped. The sneer might not be on her face, but it was clear in her voice. "There's little use in denying it. Speak the truth, and we might extend some leniency."

My gaze went from Baryte to the lowest member of the council, then to my parents, who stood straight as sticks and looking as though they were sucking on lemons—or Kaya's coffee.

I refused to stand there and deny the city who had believed in me more than any of the gargoyles on the stage had.

My voice was clear as I stated, "I love it."

I fought the urge to reach out for Thane's hand, knowing the blatant display of feeling would probably get me stoned on the spot.

"Slaymore feels like home for me, in a way no other place ever has. The town is perfect, and the majority of people who call it home are hardworking and kind. I've spent the last three and a half years walking the streets of the town and the academy, and I know every inch of it." Tears threatened to spring to my eyes. I breathed deeply and lifted my chin again.

"I know I'm not how a gargoyle should be, but I think loving Slaymore has helped me to understand the value of emotion. And I... do think there's merit in forming an attachment to one's living place."

The council was silent for what seemed like an eternity, gazing at me unblinking and unsmiling. It was as though they'd turned to their stone gargoyle forms, except they were still flesh.

Baryte broke the trance with an incline of his head. "Thank you for your honesty, Vela Kyanite. We must confer on what you have said."

He made a small circular motion with his hand, and the council turned inward, spreading their wings to give them privacy while they discussed my fate. I was standing alone on the stage, being openly gaped at by anyone who wasn't part of the council.

Mother and Father looked as murderous as emotionless gargoyles could manage. I couldn't help but wonder if they, too, had emotion, but just the negative ones, and were much better at hiding them.

The princess and her father looked at me with frank interest while her mother spoke quietly with one of her ladies-in-waiting. Thane's mother gazed about the theater as though all of Slaymore were beneath her.

"Well, this certainly explains a lot," came a voice from behind me.

I turned to find Headmistress Losia.

She gave me a wry smile. "My apologies, Vela. I should have realized."

"How could you have guessed I'd built a connection with Slaymore when I didn't even understand what was going on myself?" I asked.

"It's my job to understand my paranormal students," she replied, tucking her hands inside her sleeves. "Most of you are still undergoing change and still new to being adults when you arrive at Slaymore. It's a difficult time for everyone—a rocky time, some might say." She chuckled a little.

My brow creased. "I don't get it."

Losia shook her head. "I suppose you wouldn't, with your famed gargoyle humor. What I mean is, I should have been on the lookout for any issues you were facing. I should've spoken more frankly with Professor Carnelian, but I suppose I thought he would come to me if he considered either of you to be in any real danger…"

Anxiety spiked through me. Even if the Gargoyle Council didn't hold me responsible for Carnelian's state, would Losia?

"I'm sorry." I bowed my head and closed my eyes for a minute to stem the flow of tears.

"Whatever for?" Losia asked.

Lifting my head, I murmured, "For the professor. If I hadn't—"

Losia held up a hand. "None of that. Professor Carnelian's journal makes it evident he knew what was happening. It's also clear this is not a normal occurrence, even for your kind. He made the choice to inform no one and instead documented what was happening in a sort of hands-on experiment.

"Carnelian knew that as your bond with Slaymore grew, it would force him to surrender his guardianship, even though it meant his death. I don't know if he fully thought things through, but he was, perhaps, the only one of us with any power over this situation." She patted my arm and smiled. "So when he wakes up, let's all blame him, all right?"

The warm flush of hope blossomed inside me. "You think he'll wake up?"

"I hope so." Her smile turned a little sad. "We're doing all we can."

The council turned to face me as one entity, and Losia patted my shoulder before moving back.

"We have finished discussing. Come forward, Vela." Baryte's voice echoed around the room.

"What are you going to do to her?" Thane asked, a low rumble emanating from his chest.

There was a long pause.

"We fail to see how this is your concern," Baryte told him, a touch coldly.

Thane bristled, a pulse of violent energy rippling through the air surrounding us.

"It's okay," I assured him, then hurried to stand in front of the council before he could start some sort of inter-paranormal incident.

"Hold out your hand," Baryte instructed, and I did so, turning my palm up.

Baryte rested his weathered palm on top of mine. His long, claw-like fingernails curled around my hand.

He drew a deep breath, and as he exhaled, I felt a strange, prickling warmth spreading through my hand. It intensified until I was sure needles were jabbing through my skin.

I sucked in a harsh breath and tried to pull away, but his free hand closed about my wrist in a bruising grip. Pain exploded inside me, and I cried out before I could stop myself.

A roar came from beneath the theater, and the building trembled on its foundation as the overhead swung wildly from side to side.

CHAPTER
21

VELA

"*top!*" Losia roared in a tone that promised fire and brimstone if her command was ignored.

Baryte stiffened, but he seemed unperturbed by Losia's outburst. Instead, he looked about the trembling theater with a considering gaze.

He took in the paneled walls, the stage, and the red-backed chairs. And then he took in me—the real me, not the skinny and nervous young woman dwarfed by a hot pink robe that made me look like I'd been playing dress-up with a giantess's clothing.

"Do you feel it?" his voice was soft as he released my hand. "Can you calm it?"

I nodded my head and kneeled. Flattening my palms on the ground, I closed my eyes and let my magic flow into the ground to mingle with the life force of the city.

The steady beat of Slaymore's heart echoed in my mind. I could feel it pulsing through all of Slaymore. The academy, the town, the woods, all the way to the shore beyond.

I sent a soothing calm into the earth, reassuring the magic that all was well, comforting my city.

"It is true," Baryte said in a raised voice so the entire council could hear. "Carnelian was correct. Slaymore is alive."

"How could we not have felt magic on this level?" asked the disdainful councilwoman. "And how could it have chosen... *her*?"

"This happened decades ago. Many of us would not have been on the council when the city came alive and chose Professor Carnelian as its first guardian. When Vela's attachment to Slaymore superseded Carnelian's, the city shifted its allegiance to her. Put simply, she loves it, and the city loves her back."

"Love is a strong word." Mother's skin was a sickly green.

"And a very un-gargoyle emotion," Father added. "I know she has her struggles, but it would take an incredible amount of emotion to accomplish something like this."

"And we are certain Vela feels no such frivolous attachments," Mother added, shooting me a look that warned me to keep my mouth shut.

"But I do love it," I told her, no longer willing to back down, regardless of the consequences. "I love Slaymore, and if we can find a way to save Carnelian, I don't see why that's a bad thing. Especially if it means I can do everything I was born to do as a gargoyle."

"Technically, yes." This came from an ancient member of the council, a bent-backed gargoyle who looked like he'd half-turned to stone already. His wings were half extended from his back, and his skin was a deep green marble shot through with gold. "But you are correct. There is the issue of the other Slaymore guardian to consider."

"There is no issue. The matter is simple." The council-woman snapped out her wings and stepped toward me. "These guardianships were formed in the usual way, but we are obliged to do what must be done to save Professor Carnelian. He is more valuable to the gargoyle community and can contribute more than one who has been imperfect and flawed from birth. Vela must be removed from Slay-more at once."

My heart twisted, and bile rose in my throat. But I nodded. This seemed like the only way to save my profes-sor. He would survive, and the city would still have him. I knew my heart would never recover, but I accepted that.

"To completely break the connection, I believe it would be prudent to collar you until the bond between Carnelian and the city has healed and grown stronger." Baryte's voice sounded as though he were talking about where to eat dinner, not discussing imprisoning me.

They'd agreed I'd done nothing wrong, yet they were still going to punish me.

"Please, don't." My voice shook, and Thane was at my

side in an instant, his arm encircling my waist and keeping me upright.

"Don't bring more dishonor to your species with a show of your infamous emotions." The councilwoman motioned for someone to bring her the dreaded marble case. "This is the logical solution. It will give the council time to confer with Carnelian regarding this experiment and how to manage situations such as these in the future. It shouldn't take more than a century or two to set up the necessary contracts and safeguards."

A century or two? I'd never heard of a gargoyle being collared for that long. They'd stooped to a new level of unfeeling cruelty.

Searching the eyes of the council, understanding dawned on me. "You're scared of me."

Baryte scoffed. "Don't be dramatic."

"No, it's true. This would mean big changes within our community. Gargoyles would have to accept emotions as a strength rather than a weakness." I stood taller, like a queen in all her feathered glory.

"You're delusional," the councilwoman spat, her eyes tightening with the faint signs of rage. "You are the weakest person in this room."

Thane's snarl wasn't human and sent a lick of fear up my spine and heat between my thighs. This really wasn't the time to get turned on.

"My emotions have made me stronger than you could imagine. I will leave Slaymore. I will even fly to the other side of the world, but I will not be collared."

The councilwoman lifted the heavy iron collar from the case. "Your insolence will be punished by an additional fifty years of stone."

Thane shoved me behind him, hiding me from the council's view. "What is she saying, Vela? Tell me she isn't saying what I think she is," he hissed over his shoulder.

How could that voice still melt me, even in crisis? I couldn't stop an errant tear from sliding down my cheek.

Why couldn't I have met him earlier so we could've had more time?

"Move, beast. This is none of your concern," Baryte ordered.

"No," Thane snarled.

The single word was garbled as though not spoken with human vocal chords, and a scorching heat caused the air to shimmer around his body.

"I agree, Thane." Losia was using her normal speaking voice again, but it was sharp and made it clear she wasn't open to argument. "There must be another way to cure Professor Carnelian without uprooting Vela. She should be allowed to finish her semester here if she wishes."

"You care more for this one student than your entire academy?" the disdainful councilwoman asked sharply. "These are our customs, and you ought to respect them. As for you, dog, you ought to mind your own business."

I shoved in front of Thane, ready to take her on for insulting him, but was stopped when Thane's arm snaked around my waist and yanked me against his chest. Hard.

"Vela is my business." Thane bared his teeth. The light

gleamed on the sharp white fangs, and I wondered if they had always been that long and scary-looking.

Baryte's voice was calm but no more understanding as he extended his hand to me. "Come with honor, Vela."

"Touch her, and I'll rip your arm off, Stonehenge," Thane growled. His arms turned to steel bands around me until I was struggling to breathe.

It was a good thing I could hold my breath for a long time.

"Enough." A shrill, high-pitched voice made us all turn to look at the other side of the stage to find Thane's mother striding toward us.

The color was high in her cheeks, and her golden eyes were bright with anger as she glared at Thane. "You overstep your place, and you're embarrassing our masters. Fall back."

"No." Thane's laugh was harsh and slightly bloodthirsty.

I was still getting used to emotions and feelings, but even I could hear the underlying warning in his tone.

They needed to back off, or they were going to—I tried to remember the phrase Meri used when threatening anyone who crossed her—was it dick around and discover? That didn't sound quite right, but it was accurate.

"Insolent boy." Thane's father stalked forward, his teeth bared to display canines that seemed too long for his mouth. "What's wrong with you?" he hissed, casting a look at the royal family of Hades, who remained unperturbed by the unfolding drama.

My sadness morphed into rage. How could someone speak like that to their own son? Turning in Thane's arms, I rounded on his family.

"Nothing's wrong with him," I declared in a voice that sounded nothing like my own. "You're the ones who were born with something missing." My heart thudded painfully against my ribcage, but I was going to finish. "You couldn't be bothered to understand Thane. You were defective as parents and failed him throughout his entire childhood. Then you sent him off here to fix himself so you didn't have to see it."

Thane's parents closed the distance between us, eyes glowing with fury, but I wasn't finished.

"You were selfish and cared more about your precious bloodline then spending time with your son and helping him strengthen his talents. All he needed was a bit of love and support. I thought gargoyles were the world's worst parents, but most of them are better at parenting than you two." My chest was heaving as I finished, and I tried to catch my breath.

"The girl of stone grew a heart and suddenly thinks she is an expert on hellhounds?" Thane's father growled, a nasty smile stretched across his face.

Behind him, Thane's princess shifted from foot to foot, looking deeply uncomfortable, but the Lord and Lady of Hades watched impassively.

"Opened your legs for my son, and you think you've cured all his ailments?" Thane's mother laughed. The cruel sound echoed thanks to the acoustics of the room.

I winced, but it was the Gargoyle Council who recoiled as though literal shots had been fired.

"Perhaps you think the both of you are so defective that you can ride off into the sunset together? I should think that gargoyle logic would tell you this, girl: without our powers, we're nothing. None of us. Nothing more than pathetic mundanes with a glimpse into the life we should've had," Thane's father snarled.

Thane's lips brushed my ear. "I'm going to send my magic into you. Like the night I tried to take away your feelings. Okay?"

I nodded my agreement, trusting him and willing to give him whatever he needed. The first tendrils of Thane's magic slid through me and immediately began fanning my emotions.

Wanting to give him as much as I could, I focused on how it felt to be with him and how my heart felt drawn to him in ways I still didn't understand.

Turning to face him, I went up on tiptoe, pulling his face close to mine.

"Whatever happens tonight, I need you to know this. I love you. My heart will always belong to you." Closing the distance between our lips, I kissed him.

I didn't care who was watching or how many more years of stone the council would punish me with. All that mattered was making sure Thane knew he was loved.

Our magic arched between us. At first, the magic simply swirled and danced, like two lovers flirting, but that didn't last long. Within seconds, our two magics collided with a force that made my ears pop.

It all happened in less than thirty seconds, but that was enough time for the councilwoman to leap into action.

Rushing forward, she snapped the collar around my neck and quickly locked one of the two iron locks. A scream ripped from my throat as the collar's spell activated and forced me to my knees.

I grabbed the collar, trying to yank it off, but my fingertips were already turning to stone. Had the second lock been secured as well, my shift would have happened in the blink of an eye. Instead, it was turning me to stone in the most slow and agonizing way possible.

The councilwoman lunged forward, trying to fit the key in the second lock.

"Please. Don't," I begged through clenched teeth.

Spreading my wing, I blocked her path, then watched in horror as my leathery wing froze in position as it turned to stone.

I turned to look at Thane, wanting to tell him I loved him one last time and stared up at him in shock.

Holy freaking fluorite!

Thane's eyes shifted from dull orange to bright red to a sparkling yellow. I knew I was seeing the fires of Hades in his eyes.

A shiver coursed down his body, followed by a second and then a third. It was on the third ripple that dark fur sprouted along his skin.

Dropping to all fours, Thane's body convulsed.

"No!" I sobbed, reaching a hand toward him, only to have it turn to stone before I could touch him.

Needing to help him but powerless to move, I sent my magic through the earth beneath me. As it surged up into Thane's body, the muscle tremors eased.

Moments later, his legs lengthened, and his spine curved. I watched in awe as his beautiful face elongated into a snout and his jaws parted, revealing razor teeth and a long tongue.

Thane rolled onto his four paws and stood. He shook out his glowing coat of sleek, raven black fur, and all I could think was, *can I pet that dog—er, hellhound?*

The most shocking thing was his size. I'd seen werewolves in their wolf form. They were impressive and nearly twice the size of a natural wolf.

I realized I'd never seen a hellhound shift, though. Thane's size was jaw-dropping. He was the length of a car, and even on all fours, he was eye-level with his parents. At first, I thought all hellhounds were large, but from the corner of my eye, I watched as his parents took a step back.

While everyone was distracted, the councilwoman grabbed my collar and inserted the second key.

Before she could turn it and turn my body into a prison for the next few centuries, Thane's jaw clamped around her. Everyone gasped as he shook the councilwoman like a doll.

She must have believed she could stop the attack by turning to stone, but the instant she shifted, Thane tossed her into the air and let her crash into the floor. It happened so fast she didn't have time to shift, and the stone gargoyle shattered into pieces and rolled across the floor.

Thane stepped over me, covering my body with his as he turned a slow circle, snarling and snapping his jaw in warning. I couldn't see much, but there was no whisper of movement or even the sound of breathing.

CHAPTER 22

VELA

"No one moves. You have brought this on yourselves through stubborn pride," Losia ordered, her voice shaking with barely contained rage. "If you attack either of them, I will see that you are dragged in front of the paranormal courts in pieces."

Thane huffed, and sulfur-scented smoke curled from his nostrils. Once he was satisfied no one was going to rush toward us, he lowered his powerful jaws.

With a gentleness that should have been impossible for a beast, he bit down on the collar, crushing it with the force of his bite. The pieces of iron dropped to the floor with a loud clatter.

My shift was slow to reverse, the agonizing pain of being forced to shift having taken its toll on my body. The hellhound whined, his tongue gently licking my wings as the stone receded.

"This isn't possible!" Thane's father's angry shout broke the silence. "You've always been a weak runt. You don't have the power to wield an alpha form!"

The hellhound above me moved so fast I wondered if he'd teleported. He stopped with his nose mere inches from the elder hellhound's face.

Saliva dripped from Thane's mouth, hissing where it hit the floor and sending smoke rising toward the ceiling.

Still weak from the punishing magic of the collar, I pushed to my feet and stumbled to Thane's side. Curling my fingers in the fur of his powerful front leg, I used him to stay upright.

"Maybe power's not as rigid as you think it is." I stared his father down, my eyes blazing. "Perhaps magic chooses those who are truly worthy to possess it."

In response, the steady heartbeat of Slaymore grew stronger beneath my feet until the ground rumbled. Outside, thunder clapped, and wind slammed against the side of the hall, whistling an eerie melody.

The hellhound dropped his head, bumping my cheek with his snout. I placed a soft kiss on the top of his leathery nose.

"Lord?" Thane's father asked, looking toward his master on the stage.

For his part, the Lord of Hades seemed as emotionless as a gargoyle. He shook his head once, and with a snarl, Thane's father backed down.

"Eliana," said the Lord of Hades in mild rebuke. "I know you're bored, but enough with your games."

Princess Eliana put up her hands. "I didn't do this." Her lips pursed in thought, and a calculating glint sparkled in her eyes.

"Thane cannot shift without your permission," the Lord of Hades reminded her. "And you alone can make him change back. I'm not falling for your pranks."

"He cannot change without the permission of the one to whom he has been bound," Eliana countered, a smile playing at the corner of her mouth. "And I think, maybe... he's bound to Vela?"

I gazed up at Thane in wonder. Were we truly bound?

His eyes were the same, I realized, as they slowly changed from yellow back to a familiar ruby red. Stroking his haunch, I was delighted to find the fur was just as soft as I'd suspected.

"How would that be possible?" Thane's mother growled as though frustrated he'd let them down again.

"There hasn't been an alpha in several centuries, and no one suspected Thane could be one. Alphas are known for being overly protective, and I think his instincts were triggered when he shifted as a child to protect me. I think our bond was an accident." Eliana shrugged. "That instinct was triggered again when he was desperate to protect Vela."

She was smiling at me, I realized, and I offered her a tentative smile back.

"But he was already bound to you!" Thane's father half shouted in frustration.

"You'll watch your tone when speaking to my daughter," the Lord of Hades warned in a deadly calm tone.

Thane's father bowed, red-faced.

The Lord of Hades turned to me. His eyes were the deepest black and seemingly bottomless. It was hard to look at them for long.

I tried to curtsy, but my legs were wobbly, and the stupid robe kept wrapping around my legs. If it hadn't been for Thane catching me on his muzzle and steadying me, I would have face-planted. The hellhound chuffed softly, and I suspected he was laughing at me.

"It is possible that the extended absence from the Underworld has weakened the hellhound's connection to my daughter," he said. "Weakened it enough, perhaps, that the magic sought another one to protect. Maybe his lessons with Professor Carnelian assisted in his own magical development, and his new powers brought about this change. Either way, it's unsettling." He drummed his fingers on his chin. "Would you ask Thane to retake his human form, please?"

I didn't really want to ask Thane to do anything he didn't want to do.

Stroking his fur, I whispered, "It's all right. You can shift back if you're ready."

Thane growled a final warning in his parents' direction, then dropped to his belly and convulsed again. His skin rippled and became smooth as his form shrank.

A few moments later, he was on his hands and knees on the ground. He got to his feet, dusting himself off.

"Believe it or not, it's not a very comfortable form to stay in." He gave me a lopsided grin.

His father was glaring at him, but Thane stood tall and glared right back. I was afraid they'd get into a real fight this time, but before anyone could say something stupid, Baryte came forward.

His hands were folded before him, and beneath his calm mask, I could see unease flickering in his eyes. "I realize this situation has, perhaps, grown more complicated. But I'm afraid it has also made one thing quite clear. Vela Kyanite, while you cannot be forced to stone, you must be removed from Slaymore immediately."

"No." The single word was thick with all the savage anger Thane had probably been reserving for his father. "Vela is my soulmate. Listen carefully because I will not repeat myself again. I will kill anyone who touches a hair on her head."

Soulmate. I repeated the word in my mind and felt the pieces click into place. That was the pull I'd felt. He was my other half.

The gathered gargoyles looked as though they were going to be sick, while the royal family and entourage were speechless.

"I suggest you listen and back away from Vela. Hell-hounds are unstable around their soulmates, especially the newly mated ones. In fact, Thane has shown an incredible amount of control. Any other alpha would have already slaughtered everyone in this room. It seems his training has been more than successful." The Lord of Hades stood. "It's rare for a hellhound to find a soulmate and even more intriguing for an alpha to claim another species. I don't know what is going on here at Slaymore, but it is fascinating."

Baryte wasn't ready to cave. "The city reacted to her distress. If it did so again, the consequences could be disastrous. Vela must be removed from this place. If you won't come quietly, we will bring you by force."

He spoke calmly, but somehow, I didn't think he believed what he said.

I wondered if he could take me. He had the full power of the Gargoyle Council behind him, but I had Thane and an entire city ready to fight for me.

However, Baryte wasn't entirely wrong. If I wanted to save Carnelian, I had to leave.

"I think I might have a solution." Princess Eliana stepped forward.

Baryte looked as though he wanted to dismiss her, but protocol demanded that he bow instead. "I am open to the wisdom of the royal family."

"Well, gargoyles don't just protect cities, right? They sometimes protect individual buildings, and sometimes they also protect people? Important people?"

"Occasionally, a gargoyle is selected to guard an individual." Baryte inclined his head.

"Then Vela can be my guardian. If she agrees, of course," Eliana said. "Since Thane's not bound to me anymore, which leaves me without a permanent bodyguard. Gargoyles are tough and strong, plus she can fly, which could definitely come in handy in a crisis. If Vela's assigned to guard me instead of Slaymore, then the city should be safe, right?"

"Forgive me, but this sounds absurd," my mother broke in, her voice tight.

Baryte, however, appeared to be considering her suggestion. He tapped his chin with one claw. "If Vela is bound to you, Slaymore should revert to her old guardian and revive her bond with Professor Carnelian. This would also solve the conundrum of finding a city that would be suitable for Vela."

Ah yes, where to banish me to. It was a conundrum that would have the council arguing for months if I knew them.

"No gargoyle has ever set foot in the Underworld," my father objected.

"I won't be going there as one of the dead," I pointed out. "Come, Father. Isn't this a prestigious enough assignment? Does it not demonstrate the success of my education?"

He looked like he wanted to scowl at me, but he fell back, trading a glance with Mother. I gave them both a wide smile.

Thane's mother crossed her arms. She looked like she was ready to spit venom. "The lords and ladies of the Underworld have always had hellhound guards. Princess, if you lack a guard, please consider our other son. Thaddeus has been trained for this since the day of his birth. And as you know, he was always intended for you."

At his name, Thaddeus started and pushed himself

away from the wall. He hadn't been paying attention to any of the drama, preferring instead to study the curtains, floor, and even lighting rigs of the stage.

Eliana gave him a once-over. "No, thanks."

Thane's mother looked like she wanted to give the Princess of Hades a round slap. Eliana winked at me, and happiness bubbled in my belly. I could see the appeal of having a friend like her.

Eliana turned to the Lord of Hades next. "Dad, this would be great! I'd have two bodyguards. Vela will protect me, and Thane will protect us both. This way, he'll be fulfilling his contract as a protector of the Underworld. And I know that just knowing I have a gargoyle bodyguard would deter some people." Her eyes shone with excitement.

The Lord of Hades leaned down and put a hand on her shoulder. "My child, there is one whose permission you have not yet asked." He turned his head, and his inky black gaze fell on me.

I stepped forward, with Thane at my side, as though he was already my guardian. The irony of a gargoyle having a guardian had me biting the inside of my cheek to keep from giggling.

Eliana folded her hands and drew herself up, easily pulling some of her father's regality around her like a cloak. "Vela, I understand you have a special connection to Slaymore and appreciate the home it has given you. But I hope you'll consider becoming my guardian. I know you have a bond with Slaymore, and while we wouldn't live here permanently, you could travel here with me—and I promise we can travel through here often." She bit her lip. Was she nervous I would turn her down? "Will you do it?"

I didn't have much of a choice. But it didn't sound so bad. Traveling with the royal family of Hades all over the world?

Before the city had reached out to me, I'd dreamed of seeing the world. There were fates... and the Gargoyle Council would happily choose any one of those for me in an instant if given the chance.

Slaymore would stabilize, and Carnelian would return to full health.

Best of all, Thane, my mate, would be there with me.

"I have one condition," I said, and Princess Eliana raised her eyebrows in question. "Let us graduate."

Eliana exchanged a glance with Baryte.

"As long as we conduct the ritual of guardianship now and bind Vela to you, I believe we can put Professor Carnelian on the road to recovery," Baryte acknowledged.

His eyes locked on me. "Though you will have to be careful in the way you interact with the town. No more midnight watches. And if you see someone trying to break into a shop, call the police like everyone else."

I laughed. The sound was so bright and loud that several members of the council drew back. Baryte, however, graced me with a small, awkward smile. It was more of a grimace, but it was a start for someone who wasn't used to that sort of thing.

Thane bumped my shoulder with his and snaked his arm around my waist.

"Are you sure you're ready to put up with me forever?" he murmured in my ear.

Leaning my head on his shoulder, I blew out a sigh. I couldn't deny the pain that lanced through my heart at the thought of losing my connection with Slaymore.

Even now, the heartbeat seemed fainter than it had been just a few minutes ago. But I could feel another steady pulse calling to me... the beat of Thane's heart, just a few inches from mine.

CHAPTER 23

VELA

"**O**kay, everyone, say *magical fairy ring law* on three! Ready?" Princess Eliana held up the camera. "Thane, you're not in the picture!"

"I thought this was a 'girls only' picture," Thane grumbled.

He was dressed for the occasion in a fine blue suit with a white shirt and silver tie. Everything about him looked impeccable except for his hair, which was perfectly untamable. Just the way I loved it.

He came to stand behind me, slipping his hands over my blue graduation gown to rest on my hips.

"Three! Two! One!"

"Magical fairy ring law!" shouted Kaya, pumping her fist in the air.

She wore a green dress with a flowing skirt that practically screamed *fairy*. The rest of us settled for shouting *cheese!* Thane bent and planted a kiss on my cheek as the flash went off.

"Can the two of you ever behave?" Meri complained good-naturedly from beside us.

"No," I replied, turning so I faced him.

Tilting my head, I allowed him to capture my mouth with his own. His tongue darted between my lips, deepening the kiss.

"Okay, break it up." We parted, slightly breathless, to find Kaya brandishing her phone in front of Thane's face. "Now you can do the girl only one. And remember, you have to share Vela with us while you're here. You get to have Vela forever. The rest of us have to wait for you to visit us."

I slung my arm around Meg's shoulders and Meri's middle. Petite Kaya stood in front of us, and not even the sun shone brighter than our smiles.

We had our whole lives ahead of us, and my life looked a lot different than it had four years ago. I had a nice job with great perks, lots of travel, and Princess Eliana had become not only a good boss but a great friend.

She'd visited Slaymore a few times after the ritual of guardianship had been performed to make sure our bond was strong and to get to know me. She could party as hard as Meri, argue politics as astutely as Kaya, and cooed with Meg over Sapphire. Eliana was also the only person who had shown up for the graduation to support Thane and me.

I'd expected to feel mournful that my parents wanted

nothing to do with me since I'd spent the first two decades of my life craving their approval. Now, I realized they were more like distant acquaintances than family. And frankly, they weren't distant acquaintances I was eager to reconnect with.

Thane seemed unbothered by his parents' lack of attendance, but sometimes, I caught him staring off into the distance with a sad look in his eye and wondered if he was thinking of them. In some of my angrier moments, I enjoyed imagining what I'd do if I came across Thane's father in a dark, abandoned hallway of the Underworld.

Our future would be interesting, at least.

"Okay, I need to give my parents the grand tour," Meri said.

She looked stunning in a bright red dress that hugged her curves, and she'd placed her graduation cap at a jaunty angle.

Thane had painted all our caps to match our outfits, and Meri's depicted a bright red bird in flight. "But how about drinks later at our place? After dinner?"

"Drinks," Eliana agreed, with a little too much enthusiasm.

I shrugged. "I wouldn't mind something on the rocks."

The group groaned in unison at my lame pun. I'd been working hard to develop my sense of humor, something my roommates still hadn't gotten used to.

"One drink," Kaya said. "I'm starting the internship tomorrow."

"If Thane makes hot chocolate, I'm in," said Meg.

Thane bestowed his dazzling grin upon her. "If Meri spikes the hot chocolate, I'm in."

"*Shh!*" Meri put a finger to her lips and jerked her head.

Her parents weren't too far off, looking a little awkward on the lawn. They were even taller than Meri, standing well over eight feet and overly conscious of their massive wings and the way their claws dug into the fresh sod of the Slaymore lawn.

We watched the others head off to their families.

"I'm going back to the house, if that's all right," Eliana said. "Read a bit, and then get ready for tonight."

"Let's go." I started forward.

She laughed and put a hand on my arm. "You don't start work until tomorrow either, Vela. Relax. I'm enjoying one more day as a free agent before you're breathing over my shoulder for the rest of my life."

"But you..."

"Headmistress Losia has assured me the Slaymore safeguards are more than up to standard. I promise I'll be fine." She winked at Thane. "And you're welcome."

"You meddling in my sex life is weird. But in this instance, appreciated." Thane grinned.

Eliana replied with a jaunty wave and set off across the lawn. It was strange watching her go. I felt her in the same way I used to feel Slaymore. Except her presence wasn't as all-encompassing, nor was her heartbeat so loud. But she was always there, connected to me. I supposed that would come in handy, too, allowing me to feel if she were in distress.

"What now?" I asked Thane.

My stomach grumbled. The ceremony had been long and full of speeches, and I'd been too busy packing that morning to stop and eat.

"Well..." He took my hand and ran one finger up my arm, a sly smile creeping onto his face. A moment later, it was replaced with a much more professional and slightly embarrassed smile. "Professor!"

I turned. Professor Carnelian was walking across the lawn. He used a walking stick now, which caused a spasm in my chest. He'd never needed one before I'd accidentally almost killed him.

He came up to both of us and nodded with a sharp, birdlike jerk of his head. "I saw the princess and worried you might be called away before I could say goodbye."

"Worried? A gargoyle, worried?" Thane teased, raising an eyebrow.

Carnelian smiled. It looked as though it caused him pain to do so. "A teacher should strive to learn from his students just as they learn from him."

"Both of you have taught me a great deal, and you've learned a great deal. I'm very proud of you." He leaned on his stick and looked at me. "The city is quite put out that you're leaving, Vela. But she'll settle down again. Even though she's bonded to me, she remains fond of you."

Carnelian had called for me the moment he'd woken up, and he'd tried to explain everything in a voice like dry leaves. He'd known from the very beginning that Slaymore might bond with me the way it had bonded with him, but the more he read about gargoyle myths and ancient customs, the more he felt it was the natural order of things.

He had indeed planned to tell me everything the very night he collapsed, but he'd been unaware of how quickly the shift in guardianship would affect him. Even now, he was insistent he would've given the Slaymore guardianship to me if I'd asked, no matter what.

Sometimes, I wondered if I would have chosen to be Slaymore's guardian if his life hadn't been hanging in the balance. But with time to think it over, I'd realized that what I loved most about Slaymore were the people within it and the new family I'd made for myself. And that family was moving on now.

"It's been a pleasure getting to know you." Thane offered his hand, and Carnelian took it. "We'll visit the next time we drop by Slaymore."

"I look forward to it." Carnelian turned to me, hand outstretched, but I ducked around it and threw my arms around his middle.

He grunted in surprise, stiffening for a moment. Then he exhaled and relaxed. His arm came around my back to give it three awkward pats.

"You truly have taught me much, Vela," he said as we parted, squeezing my shoulder in a movement that seemed much more natural. "I am grateful to you."

"And I to you," I said, swallowing the lump in my throat. Was I imagining it, or were his eyes also suspiciously bright?

Carnelian cleared his throat. "I have many hands to shake, but do drop in any time."

His eye twinkled. "And when you have your pups, I expect at least one of them to be named after me."

Then he was off, leaving me red and sputtering on the lawn.

"I bet that's what he meant when he said I'd taught him things." Thane's laughter stopped abruptly. "I— Oh. Hello, Thaddeus."

Thaddeus appeared at Thane's side. He must have been hanging off to the side, waiting for us to finish with Carnelian.

It still struck me as odd how similar Thaddeus and Thane looked, yet something entirely different at the same time. Today, they were dressed equally well in their suits and ties.

Thaddeus lacked the cap and gown, though, and he'd trimmed his riotous blonde hair so that it sat close to his scalp, unable to rebel against brush or wax.

His face seemed permanently set in a faint sneer, as though he'd been emulating their mother for so long that he couldn't quite change his expression anymore.

He toed the grass. "Hi."

"Hi." Thane stuck his hands in his pockets. I instinctively moved closer to my mate. "Are Mother and Father with you?"

Thaddeus shook his head, and Thane sagged with relief. "So, what are you doing here? We can bring a message to Eliana, if that's the reason."

Thaddeus's eyes flared red with hurt. "I came to congratulate you."

"Oh." Thane scratched the back of his head, knocking his cap loose. He carefully adjusted it. "Consider me congratulated, then."

When Thaddeus remained silent, Thane offered me his arm. "Did you say you were interested in lunch?"

"Okay, wait. Ugh." Thaddeus ran a hand over his face. "I'm not good at this. But I want to be."

A guarded look slid into Thane's eyes. "Good at what?"

"Good at talking to you," Thaddeus blurted out. "Look, Thane. Our parents were awful. They were horrible to you, but they were also good at making me feel like nothing. Blaming me for letting Eliana be bonded to you and not me. And, well… you got out of there. Now you've made a good life for yourself, and your powers got better when you weren't around *them* all the time… You've inspired me."

"Are you planning to enroll here at Slaymore?" Thane asked, raising his eyebrows.

Thaddeus shook his head as he looked around. "I'm not really a study guy. I'm just going to travel. Go see the world for a bit. Maybe there's some other princess out there who needs guarding, you know?"

Thane watched him for a long moment.

Thaddeus swallowed, and I caught a brief flash of longing on his face. He was longing for someone to just acknowledge him for who he was and what he wanted. I squeezed Thane's hand.

"I think that's a great idea." Thane stuck out his hand.

Thaddeus stared at it in amazement before taking it. "I wish you luck. And remember, if you ever need to stay in one place while you figure your life out, well..." Thane glanced at me and gave me a soft smile that turned all my insides to mush. "You could do a lot worse than Slaymore."

"Thanks." Thaddeus looked down at the ground again, but now he was smiling.

I bit my lip, uncertain. Then I stepped forward and gave him a quick hug. He was family now, too. And if he could get away from his awful parents, who knew what amazing things he might accomplish?

When we were finally alone, with no more friends or family to demand our time, Thane and I set off across the lawn, hand in hand.

"What now?" I said.

"We could have lunch." Thane twirled me around, then pulled me flush against his body.

My breath hitched as his hand slid down my back. Bending down, he bent his head to give me a lingering kiss. By the time he was finished, I was panting, and it felt like fire was licking over part of my body.

"But I might like to have dessert first," he growled against my ear.

That did sound tempting. I slid my fingers over his starched shirt, pulling at a button. My hunger for food was forgotten in the sudden need to feel his skin against mine. But...

"Where, exactly, are we supposed to have this dessert?

The grounds are crawling with students, and Eliana's back at the house."

"Well..." His breath tickled my neck. "We've been together for months, and not once have we used those marvelous wings of yours to take us up somewhere private."

I laughed incredulously but found myself actually considering his proposition. "On a cloudless day? In front of everyone?"

"I've seen you use that invisibility spell more times than I can count." Thane pulled back and gave me a sly smile. "What say we put it to good use? Find out what it's like to have sex in midair? For science, of course."

"You know I can't resist sound logic." Stretching out my wings, I grinned up at him.

Scientifically speaking, it was glorious!

ABOUT DARCI R. ACULA

Darci R. Acula is Sedona Ashe's not-so-secret pen name. Sedona's books tend to focus on Reverse Harem relationships, while Darci's books feature only MF relationships.

Darci (aka Sedona) doesn't reserve her sarcasm for her books; her poor husband can tell you that her wit, humor, and snarky attitude are just part of her daily life. While she loves writing paranormal shifter reverse harem novels, she's a sucker for true love, twisted situations, and wacky humor.

Darci lives in a small town at the base of the Great Smoky Mountains in Tennessee. She and her husband share their home with their three children, adorable pup, five cats, pet arctic fox, chickens, several crazy turkeys, two chubby frogs, and over a hundred other reptiles. When she isn't working, she enjoys getting away from the computer to hike, free dive, travel, study languages, and capture images of places and animals through her photography. Darci has a crazy goal of writing a million words in a year, and spending six months exploring Indonesia.

www.darciracula.com

Starling Dax is a new name in paranormal romance! Her books tend to have action packed plots, with a side of humor, and feature MFM, RH, and MF couples.

Starling is really excited to be working on two academy series... because who doesn't wish they could attend a college filled with sexy paranormals and magic?

www.starlingdax.com

www.ingramcontent.com/pod-product-compliance
Lightning Source LLC
Chambersburg PA
CBHW030132180626
46812CB00002B/659